"I'm not letting you go, Austin," Sam said fiercely, then brought his mouth down hard on hers.

The kiss was too rough, but she didn't care. He was holding her too tightly, but she didn't care. Sobs were catching in her throat, but she didn't care.

Because it was Sam.

And then the kiss gentled. Sam gathered Austin into the warm circle of his arms and held her, making her feel more cherished than she'd ever believed possible.

She didn't want to give him up, she thought hazily. Not Sam. Not her scrumptious Sam. She wanted to spend the rest of her life seeing his smile, hearing his voice, reaching out for him and saying "Kiss me again, Sam."

But she knew it was impossible. . . .

WHAT ARE *LOVESWEPT* ROMANCES?

They are stories of true romance and touching emotion. We believe those two very important ingredients are constants in our highly sensual and very believable stories in the *LOVESWEPT* line. Our goal is to give you, the reader, stories of consistently high quality that may sometimes make you laugh, sometimes make you cry, but are always fresh and creative and contain many delightful surprises within their pages.

Most romance fans read an enormous number of books. Those they truly love, they keep. Others may be traded with friends and soon forgotten. We hope that each *LOVESWEPT* romance will be a treasure—a "keeper." We will always try to publish

LOVE STORIES YOU'LL NEVER FORGET
BY AUTHORS YOU'LL ALWAYS REMEMBER

The Editors

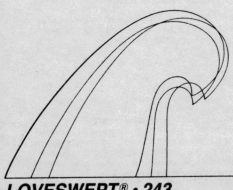

LOVESWEPT® • 243

Joan Elliott Pickart
Kiss Me Again, Sam

 BANTAM BOOKS
TORONTO • NEW YORK • LONDON • SYDNEY • AUCKLAND

KISS ME AGAIN, SAM
A Bantam Book / March 1988

LOVESWEPT® and the wave device are registered trademarks of Bantam Books. Registered in U.S. Patent and Trademark Office and elsewhere.

If you would be interested in receiving protective vinyl covers for your Loveswept books, please write to this address for information:

> *Loveswept*
> *Bantam Books*
> *P.O. Box 985*
> *Hicksville, NY 11802*

ISBN 0-553-21884-0

Published simultaneously in the United States and Canada

Bantam Books are published by Bantam Books, a division of Bantam Doubleday Dell Publishing Group, Inc. Its trademark, consisting of the words "Bantam Books" and the portrayal of a rooster, is Registered in U.S. Patent and Trademark Office and in other countries. Marca Registrada. Bantam Books, 666 Fifth Avenue, New York, New York 10103.

PRINTED IN THE UNITED STATES OF AMERICA

O   0 9 8 7 6 5 4 3 2 1

For Paige, who just keeps on smiling.
Here's lookin' at you kid.

One

Tired. Damn, he was tired.

Never before, Samuel Carter decided, had he been so bone weary, so totally exhausted. Sleep. He needed sleep. Hours and hours of peaceful, blissful sleep. He didn't even know what day it was. He'd lost track of time zones somewhere over the Pacific on a flight that had been distinguished by the presence of a screaming baby who'd put an end to his plan to sleep.

He pulled the knot of his tie down another few inches, then ran his hand over the back of his aching neck. He glanced at the dashboard of his plush car, saw that the digital clock was blinking ten A.M., and remembered he would have to reset his watch . . . when he had the strength.

If he could find the way to his new old house, he thought dryly, he'd be in great shape. He'd visited the place only twice. The first time was when he came to see what his grandfather had left him in his will and instantly had been enchanted by the house. The second time was to move in a carload of clothes and personal items just before the trip to Japan called him away. Now here he was, dog tired, bleary-eyed, and wondering where in the hell he'd left that damned house.

The neighborhood he was driving through shouted money; the homes were large, the lawns perfectly manicured. *His* house stood out like a sore thumb due to lack of care. The paint was peeling, the yard was a jungle, and if he were on the right street, he wouldn't have the slightest difficulty finding it. No one in the family had even known his grandfather owned the thing. Samuel guessed that the old buzzard had taken it in trade in one of his unusual business deals, then promptly ignored it.

Well, it was his now, Samuel mused. And he had liked it the moment he'd seen it, shabby as it was. The house had seemed to embrace him, saying "Welcome home." Strange. Anyway, he was going to fix it up, set things to rights—if the neighbors didn't shoot him on sight now that there was someone to blame for disgracing their affluent block.

"Victory," Samuel said as he spotted the huge house. Lord, it really was an eyesore. Well, once he'd had some sleep—hours and hours of sleep—he'd hire someone to inspect the place and make recommendations or repairs and improvements.

Samuel yawned, pulled into the driveway, and a

few minutes later was entering the house. He shuffled across the entryway and plodded up the stairs, feeling, he decided, closer to eighty-four than thirty-four years old. Lord almighty, he was tired.

The house had come into his possession with odds and ends of furniture. It did have a marvelous hand-carved king-size bed in the master suite, where Samuel headed. He'd made up the bed with fresh sheets before his trip, and as he entered the room, the bed seemed to beckon to him.

Within minutes he'd stripped off and dropped his expensive clothes haphazardly on the thick dove-gray carpet, and fallen onto the bed clad only in his Jockey shorts. Within seconds he was deeply asleep.

In Samuel's dream it was raining. But the rain wasn't wet; it was dry, and it floated over him like petals of a flower. It was a rather pleasant dream except that the rain was beginning to tickle his nose. He was going to sneeze. If he sneezed, he might wake up, and he was just too tired to wake up. Damn rain.

It all happened very quickly.

"Achoo!"

The force of Samuel's sneeze caused him to awaken and sit bolt upright on the bed. In the next instant he registered the fact that he was covered from head to toe in a coating of white dust. In the instant after that, to his wide-eyed horror, the ceiling above the bed began to creak and moan, then start to give way.

"Holy hell," Samuel said, catapulting off the bed. And just in time.

A large piece of plaster landed with a thud where his head had rested, and there was a gaping hole in the ceiling. Samuel blinked as two long dark auburn braids swung into view, followed by the upside-down top half of a young woman clad in a blue T-shirt. Samuel's mouth dropped open.

"Hi," the woman said cheerfully. "Guess what? You have a dab of dry rot here." She paused. "Hello? Are you in there? You look like you just saw a ghost. No, actually you look like the ghost. You're covered top to bottom in plaster dust. Even so, I can tell you have a marvelous body. Just marvelous. Anyway, I'm Austin Tyler. Tyler Construction. You know, the outfit your sister hired to check the place out. You're Sam Carter, right? If you're not, I don't think you're supposed to be here."

"It's Samuel," he said in a voice he decided didn't sound at all like his own. This wasn't happening to him, he told himself firmly. It was a nightmare produced by jet lag, and he would wake up any second. He, Samuel Carter, was not standing in his bedroom nearly nude, covered in plaster dust, talking to half of an upside-down woman who had materialized through a hole in his ceiling.

Not, he admitted absently, that she wasn't an attractive upside-down woman. What he could see of her most certainly was. She had big brown eyes, a pert nose, delicate features, and a wonderful smile. He could make out small breasts pushing against the T-shirt, and those braids—now, if this were a dream instead of a nightmare, he'd undo those braids, run his fingers through her thick hair, and watch it slide from his fingers like auburn silk.

But this was definitely, most definitely, a nightmare.

"Hello? Hello?" Austin called. "Are you with me?"

Samuel jerked. "What?"

"Look, the blood is rushing to my head. Would you be so kind as to move that piece of plaster there on the bed?"

"Sure," Samuel said, doing as instructed.

"Look out below!" Austin yelled.

Samuel flattened himself against the wall as an entire body came hurtling through the hole to land, then bounce, on the bed. Austin sat up, crossed her legs Indian-style, and smiled at him.

"Hi. Just thought I'd drop in," she said. Oh, merciful saints, she thought, Sam Carter really was beautiful. Even covered in plaster dust, he was scrumptious. He was maybe six feet tall, had broad shoulders, narrow hips, deliciously muscled legs. His eyes were blue, sky blue, sunny-day blue. His hair—well, at the moment it was white, but she'd guess it was very dark to match the smattering on his legs and the curls she could see peeking through the dust on that gorgeous chest. What that man did for a pair of Jockey shorts was a sin. "You really are scrumptious," she said, her gaze raking over him.

There was something about the heat that gathered low in his body from Austin Tyler's slow scrutiny of him that told Samuel Carter that he was wide awake. This was not a nightmare. This was not a dream. This, heaven help him, was really happening.

There he stood, he realized in ever-growing horror, Samuel Carter, of Carter, Carter, and Carter, Attorneys-at-Law, one of the most prestigious law firms in Chicago. Yes, there he stood in his bedroom, half naked, covered in plaster dust, and staring at a female construction worker named Austin, who had come flying through his ceiling. Granted, she was lovely. And not very big, he now knew, having seen her jean-clad legs. But the bottom line was, things like this didn't happen to him. It wasn't acceptable. He wouldn't tolerate this. He . . . Had Austin actually said that he was scrumptious? Scrumptious? Lord. This would never do. He had a reputation to guard, a family name to protect.

"Get off my bed," he yelled, deciding that was as good a place as any to start.

"Oh, sure. You bet," Austin said. She slid off the bed and smiled up at him. He really was very tall, she thought. And those shoulders, and that chest.

"Quit looking at me like that," Samuel said. He hurried to the bed, got in, and pulled the sheet up under his arms. Leaning against the headboard, he glared at her. What that woman could do with her eyes, he fumed, should be illegal. He could feel it, the heat, coiling deep inside him, stirring his manhood and—Dammit. "Go away."

"You're paying us by the hour." Austin said pleasantly.

"I didn't hire you. I've never heard of Tyler Construction. Go away."

"Your sister hired us. Remember? I told you that. She said that you said you thought you should have someone look this place over, then you went tooling off to China."

"Japan," he said sullenly.

"Whatever. Anyway, she was being helpful while you were away, and hired us to check the house. You do have a dab of dry rot there," she said, glancing up at the ceiling.

"There's no truck outside. Shouldn't you have a truck or something?"

"Oh, we do. My brothers went to get glass. There are a couple of broken windows downstairs. We called your sister, and she said to go ahead and fix them. You weren't supposed to be here, you know. You could have given me quite a fright."

"Me? You nearly gave me a heart attack."

She laughed. "Yes, I suppose it is a bit of a shock to have someone arrive through your ceiling. I'm sorry about that."

How lovely was the sound of her laughter, Samuel thought. It danced through the air like the tinkle of windchimes. And her eyes twinkled. They really twinkled. Lord, how dumb. Nobody's eyes actually twinkled. But Austin's did. This was insane. He had to get some sleep.

"Go away," he managed to say just before he sneezed again.

"Do you have a cold?"

"No, I do not have a cold. I happen to be covered in plaster dust in case you didn't notice. I am also suffering from the worst case of jet lag I've ever had. I want . . . I demand that I be allowed to get some sleep. In short, Miss Tyler, get out of my house!"

"Oh."

"It is miss, isn't it?" he tacked on. Oh, hell, why should he care?

"Yes, it is. I'm not married. Are you?"

"What? Oh, no, I'm not married."

"That's nice," Austin said, beaming at him. "Listen, since that dust is making you sneeze, don't you think you should take a shower? I could change the sheets for you, then you could go back to sleep."

"No," he said, staring straight ahead. "I don't have the energy to take a shower. I'm going to sleep right in the middle of this mess."

"Suit yourself," she said, shrugging.

"Austin!" a deep voice boomed from the distance.

"Oh, Lord," Samuel said, gripping the sheet, "who's that?"

"My brothers are back." She cupped her hands around her mouth. "I'm up here," she shouted.

"Wonderful," Sam muttered, shaking his head. "Invite the world in here. Let's have a party."

Thudding steps preceded the entrance of a huge man into the bedroom. The man had to be a direct descendant of Paul Bunyan, Samuel decided. Lord, he was big, with the same dark auburn hair and brown eyes as Austin. Samuel considered himself a man who kept himself in excellent physical condition, but there was no way he'd ever want to take on the muscle-bound hulk who had just entered his bedroom.

"What in the hell is going on here?" the man bellowed.

Samuel glanced quickly at the ceiling to see if any more plaster was shaking loose with the force of that voice.

"Just a dab of dry rot," Austin said, smiling. "Sam, this is my brother, Houston. Houston, Sam Carter."

"It's Samuel."

Houston laughed. "You look more like the Pillsbury Doughboy." He came forward and shook Samuel's hand vigorously. "Great house you have here. Has terrific potential. We got the glass to fix those windows downstairs and . . ."

More thundering steps were heard, then another man appeared in the bedroom. Samuel blinked, then blinked again. The new addition was an exact copy of the first hulk—same body, same face, same hair, same everything. Samuel was quite certain that he was going out of his exhausted mind.

"Hi," Austin said brightly. "Sam, this is my other brother, Dallas. "Dallas, this is—"

"Hold it!" Samuel yelled, raising his hand. "I've had it. You three are a joke, right? This is a setup, a con. My whacky sister thought for some idiotic reason this would be funny, right? Well, it isn't. Not one damn bit. Do I look stupid?"

Three sets of eyes raked his plaster-dust-covered face, then his bed.

"Don't answer that," Samuel said. "Forget that

part. Do you honestly expect me to believe that you people are for real? That some mother named her children Austin, Houston, and Dallas? That there are two human mountains who look exactly alike who are supposedly the brothers of a woman no bigger than a whisper? Ha! A woman, by the way, who gets some kind of perverse pleasure out of entering rooms through the ceiling? No way. Well, the joke is over. Leave!"

Houston and Dallas looked at each other and shrugged. Austin, however, had an opinion to voice regarding Samuel's dissertation. She marched to the edge of the bed, planted her hands on her hips, and glowered at him.

"I have news for you, Mr. Sam Carter," she said. "We are no joke. We are Tyler Construction, one of the finest firms of its kind in Chicago and surrounding areas, including your swanky suburb of Westlane. You are lucky to have us here, buster. As for Houston and Dallas, they're identical twins, which accounts for the fact that they look alike. And, if I was as big as they are, I'd punch you in your plaster-dust-covered nose. As for our names— not that it's any of your business—our mother is a devoted, and I do mean dee-voted fan of John Wayne, whom she considers the ultimate Texan in his movies. We were named in his honor. And you, sir, are rude."

"Oh," Samuel said, staring at her. Good Lord, she was beautiful. He could see the quick rise and fall of her breasts beneath the T-shirt, her eyes were flashing, and her face was flushed. What fire, what passion there was in that pint-sized package. At the moment the fire was channeled into anger, but what if it turned into desire? Desire evoked by him, directed to him? He couldn't even begin to answer those questions. She was something, this Austin Tyler. The women he knew were high society, genteel, popped out of the same elegant mold. This little parcel of dynamite standing in front of him was like no woman he'd met before. Not his type, of course, but admittedly fascinating. And very, very beautiful.

"Oh?" Austin said. "That's all you have to say for yourself? No one likes to be referred to as a joke, Sam Carter."

"Samuel." He paused. "Okay, I apologize. I do. I really do. It's just that I'm exhausted, wiped out. All I wanted to do was get some sleep, then"—he swept his arm in the air—"this." He paused again. "Didn't your father object to the fact that your mother was so hung up on John Wayne?"

Houston laughed, causing Samuel to glance quickly at the ceiling again as the booming sound reverberated off the walls.

"Our mother," Houston said, "is no bigger than Austin, and our father is larger than me and Dallas. But our dad is crazy about our mom, wouldn't deny her a thing."

"She's head of the house, all right," Dallas said, grinning. "Austin inherited Mom's . . . er, determination."

"And her temper," Houston tossed in. Austin glared at him. "Look, Sam," Houston went on, "why don't you take a shower while we change the sheets on the bed, then you can get some sleep.

We'll check out the rest of the house, then leave you a bid report. We'll be quiet as mice. You won't even know we're here."

"Good idea," Austin said, reaching for the sheet.

"Don't touch that," Samuel said, clutching it tighter.

"Oh, good grief," she said, "I've already seen your scrumptious body."

"Oh?" Dallas said, narrowing his eyes.

"I nearly landed on him when I came through the ceiling," Austin said.

"Oh," Dallas said, nodding.

"All right, I'll take a shower," Samuel said, inching toward the far side of the bed with the sheet tightly clasped to his chest. "There are more sheets in that box over there." He slid off of the bed and wrapped the sheet around him. "Check the damn house, I don't care. Just do it quietly." He went into the bathroom and slammed the door, just barely managing to get all of the sheet inside.

"Whew," Houston said. "The man is a bit uptight."

"Yeah, well," Dallas said, "you would be, too, if you were that tired from having just flown in from China."

"Japan," Austin said. "Now, shoo, shoo. I'll tend to this bed. You two go fix the windows. And be quiet. I have a feeling we'll be out of a job if we wake Sam again once he gets back to sleep. Go."

In the shower Samuel closed his eyes and allowed the hot water to beat against his body, realizing it was having a marvelously soothing effect on his aching muscles and jangled nerves.

If he hadn't just lived through that crazy scene he wouldn't believe it. Things like this didn't happen to him. But the Tyler trio had definitely happened. More specifically, Austin Tyler had happened. Damn, she had incredible eyes. Just the remembrance of her slow visual walk up and down his body caused the heat to stir again deep within him. Oh, yes, he'd definitely like to haul that feisty little number into his arms, cover her mouth with his, have all that fire directed at him.

Forget it, he told himself, stepping out of the shower and reaching for a towel. Those brothers of hers made Sylvester Stallone look like a wimp, and delectable as she was, she wasn't worth getting his kneecaps broken for. Besides, he'd already figured out that Austin Tyler wasn't his type. A female construction worker? With braids? Braids that could be set free, combed through by his fingers, made to float over his naked body when he . . .

"That's it. That's all," he said aloud as his body began to react to his errant mental wanderings. "Get some sleep, Samuel Carter, and forget this nonsense."

He opened the bathroom door and peered out, seeing no one. The bed was freshly made and turned back in an attractive invitation to his weary self. He tucked a towel low on his hips and crossed the room.

"All set?"

Samuel yelled in surprise, spinning around. "Austin. I thought you'd gone."

"I was just standing there. I guess you didn't see me in the shadows," she said, smiling up at him. Merciful saints, she thought dreamily, and here she'd decided that he was scrumptious when he was covered in plaster dust. Now, squeaky clean, smelling like soap, every inch of him except what the towel covered exposed to her view, he was absolutely beyond description. Never, *never*, had she been such a handsome, beautifully proportioned man. Just . . . just delicious, she decided.

"You're looking at me like that again," Samuel said gruffly, then slid into the bed, pulling the sheet up to his neck.

"Like what?"

"Like you're considering having me for dessert," he said, closing his eyes.

Sam Carter was a full-course dinner, she thought. "Surely you're used to women looking at you. I mean, heavens, you know how good-looking you are. Houston and Dallas know how good-looking they are. They have women chasing them in flocks, and they think it's terrific. I bet you have oodles of women too. Right, Sam?" She paused. "Sam?"

Austin moved to the edge of the bed and gazed at Sam Carter. The steady rise and fall of his chest told her that he was deeply asleep. She pulled the blanket up over the sheet, then resisted the urge to brush back the wet hair that had tumbled onto his forehead. His eyelashes fanned onto his cheeks, eyelashes, she knew, that would lift to reveal the most beautiful blue eyes she'd ever seen.

A funny flutter swept along Austin's spine, circled her waist, then landed in her stomach with a heated thud. She told herself to move, to go help Houston and Dallas, but her feet refused to obey the command. She just stood there, gazing at Sam, beguiled by his rugged features and utterly bewitched by his lips.

Wonderful lips, she mused. Sensuous lips. Lips that no doubt knew how to kiss with an expertise beyond her wildest imagination. How would those lips feel pressed to hers? What would it be like to be kissed by Sam Carter? Just looking at him made her feel strange: hot and cold at the same time and very aware of the contrast between her femininity and his masculinity.

Austin raised her hand, wanting to trace Sam's lips with her fingertip. Heavens, she thought, jerking her hand back. What was she doing? Even more, what was *he* doing to her? What was next? She sighed deeply and rolled her eyes the way her mother did at the mention of John Wayne. This was absurd. Sam Carter was a client, nothing more. She had to behave with professional decorum, starting right now. But, ohhh, those lips, those eyes, that body.

"Good-bye," she said, spinning around and marching toward the door. At the doorway she stopped, turned, and looked once more at the sleeping figure in the bed. "Rest well, Sam," she whispered, then left the room and closed the door softly behind her.

•   •   •

Austin found Houston replacing a window over the sink in the kitchen. She glanced around the room, noting the modern appliances, the double stainless-steel sink.

"This is a marvelous kitchen," she said.

"Yep," Houston said. "It was completely remodeled at some point. The plumbing throughout the house is good, all the wiring checks out. It's an old place, but it's structurally sound with just a few minor exceptions. It looks like someone was fixing it up, too, and ran out of money. Your Sam's going to have quite a house here."

"He's not *my* Sam," Austin said, smacking Houston on the rear end as she passed him.

"But don't you wish he were," Houston said in the form of a statement, then chuckled, the sound deep and rumbly. "After all, he has a scrumptious body."

"He's bee-yoo-tee-ful," Dallas said, coming into the room. "Do you want him, Austin? We'll kidnap him and give him to you for your birthday."

"Oh, stop, both of you," Austin said. "I'm not in the mood for your teasing."

"I don't know, Austin," Houston said. "You ought to take a serious look at this guy. He's a highfalutin lawyer; you've met his sister and you like her; he's got megabucks, and he's scrumptious. Now, I ask you, what more could you want? You're not getting any younger, you know."

"Right," she said. "I'm really over the hill at twenty-four. What does that make you two at twenty-seven?"

"That's different," Dallas said. "You have to think

about your biological clock. Even as we speak, time marches on. Sam Carter is definitely husband material, and I think you should take a closer look at him."

If they only knew how closely she'd looked at him already, she thought, swallowing a bubble of laughter. Oh, yes, she'd looked at every luscious inch that had been exposed to her view. Bee-yoo-tee-ful, just as Dallas said. Heavens, she'd not only looked, she'd nearly touched him as he'd lain there sleeping so peacefully. But these brothers of hers were getting carried away.

"Listen, you two cupids, the last guy you decided was perfect for me was arrested for tax evasion. Would you just lighten up on your matchmaking? You're lousy at it."

"That jerk was a slight error on our part," Houston said. "This Sam is top-notch. We heard all about him from his sister, and I read an article about Carter, Carter, and Carter. He's perfect."

"Houston," Austin said, "you can't pick out a husband for me like you'd choose a watermelon in the grocery store. Besides, I'm not ready to get married. I've been working with you two for six months now, and I love it. I've finally found my niche."

Dallas coughed and stared at the toe of his shoe as if it were the most interesting thing he'd ever seen.

"Yeah," Houston said, smoothing putty around the window, "you're quite a construction worker, all right. It's not everyone who falls through the client's ceiling and nearly creams the guy who's paying the bills."

"That wasn't my fault!"

"It never is," Dallas muttered.

"What?" Austin said, her dark eyes flashing as she looked at him.

"Nothing," he said, holding up his hands in a gesture of peace.

"I've done everything you two have told me to, haven't I?"

"You bet," Dallas said. "You're a good little worker, and you never complain. It's just that . . . well, sweetheart, not everyone is cut out for this type of work."

"What are you saying?" Austin whispered, her eyes widening.

"He's not saying anything," Houston said, crossing the room as he glared at Dallas. "We just want you to be happy, that's all. There wouldn't be any hard feelings if you decided this wasn't quite your cup of tea. You left those six other jobs without a backward glance."

"Because I was fired," Austin said. "Tossed out on my tush, and you know it. Six different kinds of jobs, and I blew every one. But I've learned from my mistakes. I haven't given you one minute's trouble. Right?"

Silence.

"Right?" she repeated.

"Oh, right," Houston said, nodding.

"I realize I have a problem," she murmured. "It gets in my way, ruins things for me if I'm not careful. But being different doesn't matter when I'm working with you two."

"Dammit, Austin," Houston said, "you don't have a problem and you're not different. You make me mad as hell when you talk like that."

"Let's not get started on that," Dallas said. "It just gets everyone uptight. I'll get the forms out of the truck and we'll sit down together and fill them out so that Sam knows what needs doing here and what our bid is."

"The baseboards are all nicked," Austin said. "They should be replaced."

"Check," Dallas said, heading for the door. "We'll tell him."

Houston watched Dallas leave, then looked at Austin again. "Austin, you're not different. When are you going to accept yourself the way you are? You're a warm, giving woman, with a lot of love to share. You're so damn hard on yourself. If you'd just accept the fact that you're—"

"Don't say it. Houston, I hate it, and you know it. I'm a construction worker, okay? I'm part of Tyler Construction. I belong with you guys. I fit in. I do, Houston."

He wrapped his big arms around her. "You bet your life you do, pumpkin. There will be a place for you with Tyler Construction for as long as you want it."

"Thank you, but you're smushing me."

"Oh. Sorry," he said, letting her go. "But, Austin?"

"Yes?"

"Don't run from a relationship with a man just

to prove a point, just to be able to say you made it as part of Tyler Construction. I'm afraid you might do that, and miss out on something special with someone special. Will you keep an open mind about the guys you go out with?"

"I guess so."

"Promise?"

"Well, I . . ."

"Promise me."

"Yes, okay, I promise."

"What about scrumptious Sam Carter?" he said, grinning at her.

"Don't be silly. Sam Carter comes from the upper crust. I can just imagine the sophisticated women he dates. He's wonderful to look at, Houston, but he's way out of my league."

"No one is out of your league," he said fiercely. "No one. I wish to hell you'd—"

"Shh. Enough."

"I love you, Austin. We all do."

"I know, and I love you all too. I have the best family in the world. You love and accept me even though I'm different."

"I'm going to wring your neck," he said, tugging on her braids. "Oh, Lord, you're enough to put a man into an early grave."

"But I'm cute," she said, batting her eyelashes at him.

Houston laughed. "Yeah, you're cute. Beautiful, in fact."

"I wouldn't go that far."

"Trust me, you're beautiful. I hope when I fall in

love that I find someone who has the capacity for loving the way you do Austin. I'd be a lucky man."

"Houston, what a sweet thing to say."

"Sweet?" Dallas asked as he came back into the room. "Houston is being sweet? Watch out, Austin, he probably wants to hit you up for ten bucks."

"Actually," Houston said, "I was going for twenty, big mouth."

"All right, children," Dallas said, "let's get serious. This bid has to be right on the mark. We need this job. We've got bills to pay, and the payment on the insurance for the truck is coming due."

"We're broke?" Austin asked, shock evident in her expression.

"Close, very close," Dallas said. "Everyone in construction and remodeling is feeling the pinch right now."

"Why didn't you tell me?"

"We've been worse off than this, honey," Houston said. "This slump will pass."

"But why didn't you tell me?" she repeated, looking at Houston, then at Dallas, then back to Houston.

Houston shrugged his massive shoulders. "It didn't occur to me. It's not that big a deal, Austin. We've been in tight spots before. We'll get out of this one like we got out of the ones in the past."

"But we should get organized," she said. "We should try to cut costs, trim expenses, reduce our overhead."

"No!" the brothers said in unison.

"Well, why not?" she said indignantly.

"Austin," Dallas said with a sigh, "do you remember what happened when you worked for that ad agency as a secretary? You went around telling all the top executives that they could trim their overhead if they brown-bagged their lunches."

"Well, they were spending oodles on ritzy lunches in fancy restaurants, and their profits were slipping."

"And," Dallas went on, "they explained to you that lunches were part of the trade, that they courted clients that way. But did you lighten up? Nooo. You tacked up signs all over the office like 'Have you hugged a bologna sandwich today?' and—"

"And they fired me," she said miserably.

"Right," Dallas said. "We, Tyler Construction, have nothing to trim back on. We refuse to use less than top-quality materials because our reputation is at stake. It'll pay off in the long run, you'll see. Now, quit worrying and let's get this bid written up."

The three sat down at the kitchen table and each contributed to the bid.

"That's it," Dallas said finally. "We'll leave it here on the table, and hope we hear from Scrumptious Sam."

"I shouldn't have yelled at him when he said we were a joke," Austin said. "I really shouldn't have done that."

"Don't worry about it," Houston said. "The guy is so bushed, he probably won't even remember. Let's go. I'll leave the key his sister gave us here on the table."

"I probably cost us this job by falling through his ceiling, then screaming in his face," Austin said, wringing her hands.

"Oh, you did not," Houston said, laughing. "If the price suits him, we'll get it."

As Dallas and Houston left the kitchen, Austin stayed behind until they were out of sight. She hurried to the refrigerator and opened it.

"Empty," she said. Sam had moved in a few of his belongings, she realized, had made arrangements for the utilities to be turned on, but apparently hadn't had time to shop even for staples before he'd gone to Japan.

"Austin!" Houston called.

"Coming," she answered. Tyler Construction needed this job, she reasoned. And she might very well have blown it by her acrobatic routine through the ceiling and her display of temper. Well, she was going to soothe the ruffled feathers she'd probably caused. She was a part of Tyler Construction, and she had responsibilities.

As she joined her brothers in the truck, she was smiling. The key to Sam Carter's house was tucked safely in her pocket.

Two

It was nearly five o'clock that evening before Samuel rolled over onto his back with a groan, yawned, then opened his eyes—opened his eyes to stare up at the hole in his ceiling.

The events of earlier in the day replayed in his mind, and in spite of himself a chuckle rumbled up from his chest and a smile appeared on his beard-roughened face.

His homecoming had definitely not been dull, he thought wryly. It wasn't every attorney who returned from a grueling business trip to have a beautiful woman fall through his bedroom ceiling. Austin Tyler. She really was extraordinary. There had been nothing wanton or offensive about the way she'd looked him over. It was as though she sincerely appreciated what she saw.

But, Samuel thought, his body had reacted to

her perusal like a match set to dry timber. If he responded like that to Austin's great big, brown eyes making a slow journey over him, he could well imagine what it would be like if she touched him; her hands roaming where her eyes had been. And kissed him; her lips following the path of her hands.

"Oh, Lord." He moaned, as heat shot through him. Knock it off, Carter, he told himself.

But if Austin were next to him in the bed, he'd—

"Shut up," he said aloud. He was hungry, he decided, shifting mental gears. Starving, in fact. He needed food.

He swung his feet to the floor, then ran his hand over his chin. He'd have to shave, he supposed. He'd rather just throw on some clothes and go out to get something to eat, but it wouldn't do for him to be seen looking like a slob. Appearance was extremely important in his profession. People had to have confidence in their attorney at all times, whether sitting in his office or bumping into him in a fast-food restaurant.

Samuel glanced up at the ceiling again and smiled. That little episode would shake up a few folks he knew, he thought, his father included. His father would be mortified if he'd witnessed the goings-on in the bedroom with Austin. Shocked. The old boy would turn purple. Now, his grandfather, rest his soul, who was the original Carter of Carter, Carter, and Carter, would have loved every minute of it.

The law firm. If it was to go on, Samuel's father had said after the funeral, then Samuel had to produce an heir. Hadn't it occurred to anyone that a child of his might not want to be an attorney? he wondered. No, of course not, it was simply assumed that was how it would be, as it had been when he was growing up.

Which was fine for him, he reasoned, because he enjoyed his work. Being a corporate attorney specializing in contract law was exciting. Scratch that. It wasn't exciting. It was . . . challenging. Yes, that was the word he wanted. He was highly respected in his field. He was his father's son, and proud of it. He moved in the moneyed circles of society, attended the symphony, the theater, benefits with women of wealth and breeding on his arm. He bedded a few who weren't looking for commitment, and treated them all with respect.

But not one of them had ever said that he was scrumptious.

"Oh, for Pete's sake," he said, striding into the bathroom.

A short time later Samuel was clean-shaven, dressed in gray slacks and a yellow dress shirt open at the neck, and was definitely aware that his stomach was empty. He was so hungry he was imagining that he smelled the tantalizing aroma of cooking food.

As he walked along the hall, then made his way downstairs, the aroma grew stronger. His sister? he wondered. Had Marilyn come over to fix him some dinner? No, she didn't even know he was back from Japan, as he hadn't really been expected until tomorrow. Then, who . . .

Samuel quickened his step and hurried into the kitchen.

And then he stopped dead in his tracks.

In front of the stove, whose every burner was covered with a pot or a pan, was Austin Tyler. His gaze swept over her. The braids had been transformed into a gorgeous waterfall of auburn hair that tumbled nearly to her waist. Her splendid figure was set off to perfection by a perky blue sundress. Shapely legs flowed down to pretty feet encased in sandals from which delicate toes, their nails pink with polish, peeped out. His gaze took in all of her, every inch, and the blood pounded in his veins.

"What—" he started, then stopped as he realized he'd croaked out the word. He cleared his throat and tried again. "What are you doing?"

Austin looked over at him and smiled. "Hi, Sam," she said brightly. "You look great, very well rested. Did you sleep like the dead?"

"It's Samuel," he said crossly, walking toward her. Lord, what fantastic hair. He wanted to sink his hands into it now. Right now! "Yes, I slept very well, considering how my day here started out. But you didn't answer the question. What are you doing, Austin?"

"Cooking your dinner."

"Why?"

"Well . . ." She sighed. "I'm terribly sorry about falling through your ceiling, then yelling at you because you said we were a joke. So I decided to make it up to you, sort of wipe the slate clean. It's not fair to my brothers that we might not get the job remodeling this house because of things I did. I was hoping that I could make amends so you could consider our bid with an open mind. Okay? Are you hungry? Oh, you must be, you slept the day away. Well, I'll have a dinner in front of you in a flash. You just sit down there—"

"Hold it!" Samuel said, slicing his hand through the air for silence. "Don't you ever run out of oxygen?"

Austin blinked in surprise.

"Occasionally, I mean—"

"Austin," he said, interrupting her again, his tone gentling, "it wasn't necessary for you to go to all this trouble. It wasn't your fault that you fell through the ceiling. I'm just glad that you landed on my bed so you weren't hurt. And as for the other, I shouldn't have called you a joke. So, you see, there are no amends to be made."

"There aren't?" she said, frowning.

"No."

"Well, mercy, what am I going to do with all this food? This is my peace offering."

"It smells terrific," he said, smiling at her. "It would be a shame to have it go to waste."

"Oh, Sam," she whispered, "you smiled. That's the first time you've done that. You have the most absolutely, positively wonderful smile."

Austin's whispered words seemed to speak directly to his libido. The smile slid right off of his chin and his pulses began to race.

"Why do you say things like that?" he said, gritting his teeth. "Do I go rambling on about how beautiful your hair is? How you look like a breath of fresh air in that dress? How I'd like to haul you into my arms and kiss the living daylights out of you? Hell, no, I don't say . . ." His voice trailed off, and an expression of horror registered on his face. "I can't believe I just said all that."

Austin smiled. "Did you mean what you said?"

"Damn right, I did," he said none too softly, "but that's beside the point. What are you doing to me, Austin Tyler? I don't behave like this."

She shrugged. "I'm just fixing your dinner. Thank you for the lovely compliments. You really like my hair?"

His gaze swept over the auburn cascade. "It's incredible," he said, his voice husky. He slowly lifted his hand and wove his fingers through the tresses, watching it slide back into place like silken threads. "Incredible," he repeated.

Austin's gaze met his, held . . . and the room disappeared. Samuel stepped closer to her and framed her face in his hands.

"I'm going to do it," he said, an incredulous tone to his voice. "I don't quite believe it, but I'm going to do it. I'm going to kiss you, Austin."

"I'm glad," she said, her voice tremulous.

"Are you?" he said, lowering his head toward hers. "I wouldn't want to offend you, or upset you, or—"

"Kiss me, Sam."

"Right."

The kiss was warm and soft and sensuous. It seemed to steal the breath from Austin's lungs and make her body hum with joy. The kiss was a sensual promise of more to come, and she responded in total abandon. She wound her arms around Sam's neck and parted her lips to receive his tongue that sought entry to her mouth with gentle insistence. The kiss was like none she had ever experienced before, and she was sure she would die from the sheer beauty of it.

Heat churned within Samuel as he filled his senses with the taste, the aroma, the feel of Austin. He drank her sweetness like a thirsty man. His hands slid to her back, weaving beneath her heavy hair to press her to him, to fit her slender curves to his hard body that was aching for more of her. A soft purr escaped from her throat, and the passion-laden sound caused a flash fire of desire to ignite within him. He plummeted his tongue deep into her mouth as the kiss intensified.

Dear Lord, how he wanted her.

Never before had he been swept away on a tide of sensations like this. Control, he thought hazily. Where was his control, his restraint, his gentlemanly behavior? He was lost, gone, slipping over the edge. He had to stop. Now!

Samuel jerked his mouth from Austin's and drew a raspy breath. He nearly groaned aloud as he looked at her, seeing her eyes that had drifted closed, her moist, slightly parted lips, the flush of passion on her cheeks. With every ounce of willpower he could muster, he forced himself to take a step back.

Austin slowly opened her eyes as her arms floated from around his neck. She met his gaze and smiled.

"Oh, my," she said wistfully. "Oh, Sam."

"I'm sorry," he said, raking a restless hand through his hair.

"You are?" she asked, her eyes widening. "You're sorry that you kissed me? Why? I thought it was wonderful."

"It was."

"Then why are you sorry?"

"Because I got carried away," he said, his voice rising. "Because I wanted more. I wanted to take off your clothes and bury myself in you, make love to you until dawn. Because I lost control, dammit."

Austin laughed. "My goodness, Sam, you're certainly upsetting yourself. I wanted to tear off all your clothes, too, but neither one of us did it, so what's the problem?"

"You did? You wanted to tear off my clothes?"

She turned back to the stove and peered into a pan. "Oh, my, yes. I've never been kissed like that before. It was sensational. Funny little things were happening inside me." She looked at him again. "There was such need in me, and my breasts felt so heavy, which is weird because I haven't got much there to become heavy. And then—"

"Oh, please," Samuel moaned, dropping his face into his hands, "no more. Don't say another word. I can't handle this."

"Sam?' she said, leaning slightly toward him.

He moved his hands to grip her upper arms. "Austin, you can't go around saying things like that to a man who is a breath away from taking you right on the kitchen floor. Understand?"

"You wouldn't do that." She glanced at the floor, then back at his face. "Would you?"

"Don't press your luck. I don't seem to act true to form around you. I don't know what you're doing to me. I don't lose control. I simply don't allow it to happen."

"That doesn't sound like much fun," Austin said, frowning. She turned and began to ladle food into serving dishes. "Well, I suppose you don't have much choice in the matter." She carried two dishes to the table. "There were odds and ends of crockery and utensils here, Sam. Nothing fancy, but certainly usable. You don't have dining room furniture, so I hope you don't mind eating in here."

"You're joining me, aren't you?"

"Sam, I don't—"

"Please?"

"Okay. I'm a terrific cook, and I love to eat what I whip up. We're having pork chops with candied apple rings, baked potatoes, and baby carrots. There's marble cake for dessert."

"Fantastic," he said, sitting down at the table. Austin served and, seated across from him, watched as he took the first bite. "Delicious," he said.

"I know," she said, smiling. "My father taught us all how to cook. Dallas and Houston are capable of producing a full-course dinner from soup to nuts."

"Your father taught you? I suppose this sounds a bit chauvinistic, but isn't that usually a mother's job?"

Austin laughed. The musical sound caused a

shaft of heat to shoot through Samuel's body, and he quickly turned his full attention on the food.

Just chat, he told himself firmly. Don't think about that kiss. Do not think about how Austin Tyler had felt in your arms. About how Austin had tasted, much less about how she'd fit next to him as if she were custom made for him alone. No, he wouldn't dwell on the sensations of desire that had swept through him like a raging fire, or the fact that he'd wanted her like he'd wanted no woman before. He'd just chat. Fine.

"Well, you see . . ." Austin started.

"What?" Samuel said, jumping in his chair.

Austin looked at him in surprise. "You asked me why my mother didn't teach us how to cook."

"Oh, yes, of course," he said, nodding. "So! Tell me, Austin, why didn't your mother teach you how to cook?"

"Sam, are you all right?"

"Jet lag," he mumbled into his coffee mug. "Carry on with your story."

And Austin did. "My mother is wonderful," she said. "I don't know anyone who approaches life the way she does."

"What do you mean?"

"She smiles. It's hard to explain, Sam, but my mother believes that life is too short, too special, to embrace anything gloomy or upsetting. So, she doesn't. Some people think she's totally scatter-brained, but we, her family, adore her, and we're all she cares about."

"You and John Wayne."

"Isn't that cute?" Austin said merrily. "My father said we should count our blessings that she didn't have a crush on the Three Stooges or the Marx Brothers. Anyway, she decided that cooking was ridiculous because a person spends hours preparing food that is gobbled up in minutes, so what's the point? My father said 'Okey-dokey' and took over the kitchen. In exchange, my mom does the yard. She likes that because her labors produce flowers she can enjoy for a long time. She always looks at the bright side. When Dallas broke his arm when he was ten, she said he should be glad it wasn't his head, then she drew happy faces all over his cast with colored markers."

"I think she sounds like a very rare and lovely person," Samuel said gently.

Austin met his gaze. "Yes . . . she is," she murmured. Oh, mercy, she could scarcely speak, or think, or breathe when he looked at her like that. She wanted him to kiss her again. She wanted to say "Kiss me again, Sam," then crawl onto his lap to feel his mouth claim hers, his tongue find hers, his hands roam over her. Oh, it had been heaven to be in Sam's arms. She'd never been kissed like that before, or felt like that before, or wanted so much, so very much more.

Samuel cleared his throat and switched his gaze back to the food on his plate. They ate in silence for several minutes.

"Austin," Samuel said finally, "could we back up a bit? You said that you guessed that I didn't have much choice in how I conduct my life. What did you mean by that?"

"Are you the third Carter in Carter, Carter, and Carter? I assume that you are."

"Yes. My grandfather, who just passed away and left me this house, was the first. He was something. He'd put together a hundred-thousand-dollar deal and seal it with a handshake. My father and I would corner him and insist that contracts be drawn up and signed."

"Why?"

"Why? Lord, Austin, things have to be done properly, legally. Every clause, every detail has to be gone over very carefully. My father impressed upon me from childhood that a man must always be in control of his mind, of what he's doing, so that he has the edge over the competition."

"And as the third Carter, you followed in his footsteps, using his philosophy rather than your grandfather's."

"Well, yes, of course."

"Did anyone ever try to cheat your grandfather between the time he shook hands on a deal and you could scramble around to get signatures on legal documents?"

"I . . . well, now that you mention it, no, not that I know of. The people he dealt with always seemed rather amused when they signed the contracts."

"Interesting. I'd bet your grandfather smiled his way through life, just like my mother does."

"Yes," Samuel said slowly, "I think maybe he did."

"Does your father smile, Sam?" she asked quietly.

He looked at her for a long moment. "No."

"Do you? Never mind, you've already answered that. You're the third Carter, your father's son. You said yourself that you never lose control, that there is a reason and a purpose for all that you do. In short, you keep tight rein on yourself and walk a very straight line."

"Am I being insulted?" he asked, frowning slightly.

"Heavens, no. I envy you the fact that you know exactly who you are, where you're going, what you were meant to be. You have a path from point A to point B; it's clearly defined, with no detours, no passing Go and collecting two hundred dollars. You never deviate from the plan you've mapped out for your life."

"You make me sound boring as hell."

"That wasn't my intention. I'm twenty-four years old, and I'm floundering, trying to find my place. I'm hoping, praying, that I belong with Tyler Construction, but I have niggling doubts about it. But you? You're set for life. That must be a very secure feeling."

"I guess so. I never really thought about it. I'd like to think that I'm open-minded, receptive to change and new ideas. I know I am, because I moved into this house."

"A house your grandfather left you. What did your father say about your move?"

"He thought I should get rid of this place as quickly as possible and stay in my apartment because it's only minutes from the office. Living out here in Westlane isn't very practical."

"So why are you here?"

"I don't know. There was just something about this place that made me feel welcome from the moment I stepped inside the door. My father is right, of course, I'm better off in the city."

"But you're going to fix up this house and stay?"

"Yes. Yes, I am."

"There's hope for you yet, Sam," she said, smiling. "Your grandfather would be proud of you."

"My grandfather was not my role model, believe me."

"But, Sam, he knew how to smile." She got up from the table. "I'll get you some cake."

Samuel drummed his fingers irritably on the table, his dark brows knitted in a deep frown. Dammit, *he* knew how to smile, he told himself. Austin had even said his smile was absolutely, positively wonderful.

He nodded decisively, then in the next moment shook his head. No, he admitted, that wasn't what she meant, and he knew it. He was skirting the issue, playing word games. Austin was talking about a way of life, an outlook, a philosophy for living. Hell, the world would be in a real mess if everyone went around smiling in the context that Austin meant, like her mother did and his grandfather had. It was ridiculous. Everything would fall apart; there'd be anarchy.

"It's dumb," he said aloud.

"No, it's marble cake," Austin said. "It's supposed to have two flavors swirling together like that."

"I'm not talking about the cake. I meant this

smiling philosophy of yours. I'm not insulting your mother, Austin, but if everyone conducted herself like that, and like my grandfather did, we'd be in a heap of trouble in this country."

"Oh, I agree."

"You do?" he asked, obviously surprised.

"Of course. My mother, for example, is enchanting, but I don't think she's had a serious thought in her life. We can't all do that. But we can take a lesson from those who know how to smile, mix it together with the straitlaced part of ourselves, and hopefully come up with an even blend. I'm not sure that you— Well, never mind."

"That I what?" he said, leaning toward her.

"The fact that you're in this house scores points in your favor. But I don't know, Sam. From the things you've said, I gather you're very set in your ways. Purpose. Control. Those are your key words. That's fine if you're happy. To each his own."

Happy? Samuel thought. Well, sure he was happy. Wasn't he? What was the definition of happy? For kids it was candy, puppies, birthday parties, clowns. But for a grown man it was . . . it was . . . Oh, hell, he didn't know! No, now, wait a minute. He was intelligent, he could figure this out.

"Happiness is . . ." he said, staring up at the ceiling.

Austin laughed. "You sound like all those posters and stickers that were so popular a few years ago."

"It's subjective. In the eye of the beholder." He

looked at Austin. "Are you happy? Do you blend that ability to smile with a more practical side?"

"Yes, I'm happy." She paused and fiddled with her fork, averting her eyes. "Most of the time."

"You said you were trying to find your place."

"Yes," she said, looking at him again. "I just want to fit in."

"Do you mean you haven't made a definite career choice?"

"Something like that. I'm hoping that Tyler Construction will be my answer. We'll see. Did you finish your mental 'Happiness is . . .' poster?"

"I didn't," he said. "I'm going to have to think about it."

"And I," she said, getting to her feet, "am going to clean up this kitchen."

"I'll help you, Austin," Samuel said. "Not only was the food delicious, but having a home-cooked meal was a real treat. The least I can do is help you clean up."

"It won't take long. You have a practically brand-new dishwasher here." She began to pull open the cupboards. "Now, to find some little bowls for the leftovers."

Austin zipped around the kitchen in a manner that was not conducive to conversation. There were no wasted steps in her flurry, Samuel noticed, and he stayed alert so as not to get in her way as he carried things from the table. The kitchen was sparkling clean and the dishwasher was humming in record time.

"Whew," Samuel said. "You are a dynamo. Very efficient."

"Did you notice how I set all the leftovers on the counter, then opened the refrigerator only once to put them away? That saves on electricity in the overall picture. Studies have shown that repeatedly opening the refrigerator door costs more than— Oh, forget it. This is boring."

"No, it's not, it's interesting."

"Well," Austin said, eyeing him warily, "it's true of air conditioners too. It costs more to turn them on and off than to leave them running. Sam, this is *not* interesting."

"I think it is. What other tidbits do you have in that pretty head of yours?"

"Nothing," she said adamantly. "Nothing at all." She brushed passed him and left the kitchen.

Something was wrong, Samuel realized. Austin had suddenly become upset and looked as though she were close to tears. Did she get jangled talking about refrigerators? What was going on?

As Sam started after Austin, he noticed some papers at the far end of the kitchen table that hadn't caught his attention during the meal or cleanup. He picked them up and saw they were the bid sheets from Tyler Construction. He went into the living room to find Austin staring out the front window.

"Austin?"

"I adore summer sunsets," she said, not turning toward him. "Of course, some people don't consider May as summer, but I do. You'll have a lovely yard once it's tended to, Sam. This is really a very nice neighborhood and—"

He crossed the room and stood behind her. "Austin—"

"Maybe you'll find that you like to putter in the yard. Some men enjoy that. I—"

"Austin, what's wrong?"

"Nothing."

"Turn around and look at me."

"I really must be going."

"Look at me."

She turned slowly to face him, and Samuel's heart thundered as he gazed down at her. Her eyes looked as big as saucers, her gently parted lips were moist, inviting, calling to him to claim them with his own. She seemed incredibly fragile, and incredibly sad. He didn't know why she was suddenly unhappy, but he wanted to take her into his arms, wrap her in his warmth and strength and protect her from harm.

Without really thinking it through, or analyzing the whys and wherefores, he tossed the papers onto a chair, drew Austin into his embrace, and covered her mouth with his in unhurried pleasure. A soft sound escaped from Austin's throat, and he wasn't sure if it was a sigh or a sob. He slid his tongue into her mouth to meet her tongue, and felt her hands on his back increase their pressure.

Never before Austin had he entertained thoughts of closing the door on the world and making love for hours. Hours and hours and hours. He'd never been filled with such driving want and need . . . not before Austin.

Samuel lifted his head only long enough to draw

a rough breath, then took possession of her mouth once more. He slid his hands slowly down her silken hair. His fingers inched over the gentle slope of her buttocks to fit her more closely to him. His manhood strained against his zipper—heavy, heated, wanting, aching.

And the kiss went on and on.

Austin answered the demands of Sam's mouth in total abandon—not thinking, only feeling, as a nameless yearning intertwined with a pulsing heat within her. She was suspended in pleasure, floating in a hazy mist of wondrous sensations. Reason fled; passion reigned supreme. It was ecstasy.

Samuel lifted his head once more, his breathing labored, then buried his face in the fragrant cloud of her hair.

"Austin," he murmured.

His voice caressed her, flowed over her like warm honey as she leaned her head against his chest and drew a wobbly breath. Her knees were trembling, and every inch of her body seemed to be tingling with awareness, with heat, with an indescribable sense of being alive, and wanting, needing, more of Sam Carter.

"Oh, Austin," Samuel said, releasing the deep breath he had taken. He reluctantly moved her gently away from his throbbing body, but kept his hands resting on her bare shoulders. "I can't believe what you do to me."

"Are you going to say you're sorry again?" she asked, hearing the thread of breathlessness in her voice.

"No, because I'd be lying. Are *you* sorry?"

"No," she said, smiling at him. "Oh, no, Sam, not at all."

"Austin, why did you become so sad when we were talking about refrigerators and turning off air conditioners?"

She laughed, the musical resonance having its usual disturbing effect on Samuel's heart rate. He inwardly groaned as he felt desire churn within him.

"When you put it like that," she said, "you make me sound like a nut case."

He lifted his hands to trail his thumbs back and forth over her cheeks. Austin shivered from the sensation.

"You're not a nut case," he said, looking directly into her eyes, "but you are a very complicated—beautiful but complicated—woman. Tell me, Austin. Tell me why you became so sad when we were talking in the kitchen."

"I'm just tired. I've had a busy day, you know. Falling through ceilings takes a lot out of a person. Yes, that's it, I'm totally worn out. The refrigerator didn't upset me, I'm pooped, that's all." She stepped back, forcing him to drop his hands from her face. "I must go. Where's my purse?" She glanced around.

She was doing it, Samuel realized. She was jabbering a hundred miles a minute again. He wanted to grab her, give her a little shake, demand that she stop hiding behind her blithering, and talk to him, really talk, tell him what had upset her. But he somehow sensed that this was not the time to push her. She seemed a bit frantic now, and she was avoiding looking at him.

"There's my purse," she said a trifle too loudly. She hurried across the room and snatched it from a chair. "Well, I'm off," she said, starting toward the front door. " 'Bye, Sam."

"Austin!"

The deep sensual rumble of his voice stopped her dead in her tracks, and she turned her head to look at him.

"Yes?" she whispered.

"Thank you."

"For dinner? Oh, sure, no problem."

"Thank you . . . for everything."

Austin opened her mouth to speak, closed it again, then hurried out the front door.

Samuel moved to the window and brushed back the curtain, watching as she nearly ran to her car. Darkness was coming quickly and she turned on the lights. He didn't move until she'd driven the compact car out of his view, the taillights seeming to burn his eyes as she disappeared. He drew his hand down his face, and a shudder ripped through him.

The house was too quiet. The echo of Austin's laughter was fading, leaving an emptiness, a chilling silence.

Dear heaven, what was she doing to him? he wondered. His brain, his body, his entire being, were out of control. His emotions, thoughts, his libido, were out of control.

And it was scaring the hell out of him.

"Damn," he said, shaking his head. He turned

from the window and his glance fell on the bid papers he'd tossed on the chair. He picked them up, crossing the room to turn on a light and sink onto a lumpy sofa.

He'd read them, Samuel decided, for something to do, but he already knew he wouldn't get a comparison bid. He'd hire Tyler Construction. He had no choice. He had to see Austin again.

It was the only way to regain control of himself, Samuel reasoned. He was—yes, that was it—a victim of bizarre circumstances. He'd been exhausted, had a beautiful woman fall through his ceiling, had had his existence thrown out of kilter when he was in a weakened state. He hadn't had time to recuperate before finding Austin in his kitchen fixing his dinner.

Oh, praise the Lord, he thought, he had it figured out: Control would be his again the moment he saw Austin in the light of a new day.

With a decisive nod and renewed sense of well-being, Samuel began to read the bid papers.

Three

Austin's apartment was above the two-car garage at her parents' home. Converting it into living quarters had been one of Dallas and Houston's first projects when they started Tyler Construction, and Austin was delighted with the results.

She had wondered initially if her parents would monitor her comings and goings, but they paid little attention, simply treating her as the tenant above the garage. Both her mother and father waited for her invitations before climbing the wooden stairs and knocking on her door.

After leaving Sam's house, Austin drove slowly out of the affluent neighborhood of Westlane, along the interstate for ten miles, then off to the right to the middle-class suburb of Windmill. The houses were old, the yards medium-size. It was a noisy, family neighborhood, where the Tyler clan had lived since before Houston and Dallas had been born. It was the only home Austin had ever known, but tonight it failed to make her feel warm and welcomed.

As she stood in the driveway staring at the two-story house aglow with lights, then up at her apartment that was dark and silent, Austin felt foreign, strange, as if she'd never been there before. A part of her had an urge to run inside the house, fling herself into her mother's arms, and weep. Another part of her wanted only to be alone, to go up to her place, lock the door, and never emerge again.

With a sigh she climbed the stairs and entered her apartment. After turning on a light she glanced around, taking in the bright colors, the flowered prints and white wicker furniture, the plants hanging in the windows, the old-fashioned rolltop desk against one wall. She'd chosen mint-green carpeting, and the entire effect was one of freshness, like a field of wildflowers.

Austin wrinkled her nose and slouched on the sofa. She'd managed to blank out her troubled thoughts during the drive home, but now, in the silence of her own small apartment, there was no escaping.

Sam Carter.

Scrumptious Sam.

Sam, and the way she had felt when he'd held and kissed her.

And the way she had made a complete fool out of herself over the incident about the refrigerator and turning off the air conditioners.

"Darn it," she said, punching a throw pillow. "And dammit too." Sam had to think she was crazy. Why else would she get so rattled about a refrigerator? She'd come across as certifiable no doubt about it. She usually stayed alert, being excruciatingly cautious about what she said. But she'd been relaxed with Sam, so comfortable with him that she'd let her guard down. She could just scream.

Throwing up her hands in self-disgust, she rose and went into her bedroom, which had the same cheerful decor as the living room. She changed into jeans and a T-shirt, wandered barefoot around the living room, then sank back onto the sofa with a dejected sigh.

And thought about Sam.

Such new and wondrous sensations had swept through her when he'd kissed her, she mused. She'd never felt like that before. Not ever. Sam was so strong, yet so gentle, and she'd felt protected, safe, and so feminine in his embrace. He'd evoked a level of passion within her she hadn't even imagined she possessed. Desire had hummed through her body like a joyous song awakening what had been slumbering deep within her.

Oh, it had been glorious.

And wrong.

Austin sighed again, decided she was getting very proficient at making that sad sound, then added one more sigh for good measure.

She had no business daydreaming about Sam Carter, she told herself. She shouldn't have allowed him to kiss her, nor should she have responded to those kisses in total abandon as she had. She shouldn't be sitting there knowing that if he walked through her door at that very moment, she'd fling herself into his arms and say, "Kiss me again, Sam." She shouldn't be thinking about him at all.

But she was.

And the remembrances of those kisses shared brought a flush to her cheeks, and a heat deep within her body.

And it was all so very, very wrong.

Sam was Chicago society, part of the upper crust, the three-piece-suit professionals. There was no room in his world for Austin Tyler. She wouldn't fit in there.

So, Austin thought bleakly, facts were facts. Her encounter with Sam, the kisses they'd shared, being held in Sam's arms, were stolen moments out of time. Even if Sam hired Tyler Construction, she probably wouldn't see him again. He'd be at his office while the work was being done at his house, then she'd make certain she wasn't there on the day of final inspection. No, she'd never see Sam Carter again.

And that was one of the most depressing thoughts she'd ever had.

She'd forgotten to get her mail out of the box, Austin thought suddenly. There was a good project that would take her mind off of Sam for all of five or six minutes. Whoop-dee-do, she thought sarcastically.

Austin went back outside and down the stairs, aware of a crispness to the air now that night had fallen heavily over the city. She glanced again at her parents' house, dismissed the idea of making a social call, as she didn't feel social at all, then trudged to the mailbox at the curb.

A few minutes later she was back in her living room, absently sifting through the stack of mail.

Suddenly a chill swept through her and her hand trembled as she stared at the business-size envelope. The return address seemed to scream at her for attention, insisting that she acknowledge it, recognize it for what it was, who it was, once again invading her life.

"No," she whispered, shaking her head. "No. Leave me alone." *No!* her mind echoed over and over. She wouldn't open it, she wouldn't read yet again the words that said she was different, not like everyone else. Why did they do this to her? Why couldn't they understand that she just wanted to be left alone?

She tossed the remaining mail on the sofa, then tore the envelope in shreds, dumping the scraps into the wastebasket.

She stared at the tattered paper . . . remembering. Remembering. And hating the memories.

Austin wrapped her hands around her elbows in a protective gesture as she stood mesmerized by the sight of the jagged paper as the painful memories assaulted her. The chill within her grew, causing her to tremble from head to toe as tears welled in her eyes.

She mustn't do this to herself, she thought from a faraway place in her mind. She was home. She was safe. She had to think about something else, something in the here and now that would chase away the ghosts of the past and warm the chill, the awful chill, within her. Something wonderful, special, beautiful . . .

Sam.

Austin closed her eyes and filled her senses with the essence of Sam Carter.

The chill within her was slowly replaced by a honeyed warmth that turned into desire. She savored it, welcomed it, allowed it to consume her.

Sam.

"Thank you, Sam," she whispered to the empty room, then turned out the lamp and walked wearily into the bedroom.

Tyler Construction could not afford the luxury of an office and a secretary. The office consisted of an answering machine installed in Houston's apartment, where the three-member crew met each morning to review any messages and plan their day.

How many women had been shuffled out the door before the eight o'clock gathering, Austin didn't know, but surmised that the number was plentiful. Her brothers were extremely handsome, virile men, and women in Chicago and beyond were not blind or unfeeling. The Tyler twins were also, in Austin's opinion, very nice people, who treated women with the respect due them.

When Austin arrived at Houston's the next morning, he greeted her with a smile, a cup of coffee which he shoved into her hand, and the announcement that Sam Carter had just called to say he was hiring Tyler Construction to remodel his house.

"Oh," Austin said.

"That's it? Oh?" Houston said. "Where's the shriek of joy, the smile, the enthusiasm, kid? We needed that job—*and* you'll get to see Scrumptious Sam again."

"No, I won't," Austin said, sitting down at the kitchen table. "I mean, he'll be in the city while we're working on his house. I can't picture bumping into him. Where's Dallas?"

"I don't know. He's late, which isn't like him. He was seeing Joyce again last night so . . ." He shrugged. "Do you realize that Dallas hasn't seen anyone but Joyce for over six months?"

"No," Austin said, looking at Houston in surprise. "I just assumed he was playing the field as usual."

"So did I, but he told me about Joyce yesterday. I think he kept it hush-hush because he couldn't quite believe it himself."

"You mean he's in love with her?"

"He didn't go so far as to admit that, but the signs are sure there. I like Joyce, don't you?"

"Oh, yes, she's lovely. And her little boy is adorable. He's so small for a five-year-old, but Dallas is wonderful with him. You know, he doesn't roughhouse too much, knows how to make him feel important."

"The kid has asthma, right?"

"Yes, that's what Joyce told me when we all went on that picnic. Her husband left them when the baby—his name is Willie. Isn't that cute? —anyway, when Willie was tiny the creepy husband left because he couldn't handle the thought of having a sickly child. Joyce has dealt with it alone all these years, but she's not bitter. She loves Willie so much. I think she and Dallas are a marvelous couple."

"Well," Houston said, "don't tell him I told you that he's seeing only her."

"No, I'll wait until he's ready for me to know. What about you, Houston? Anyone special in your life?"

"Nope. Why mess around with a good thing? I have all the women I can handle." He paused. "I'm also lying through my teeth, because I'd like nothing better than to fall in love, get married, and be a father. When I think about holding a baby that I helped create, I get goose bumps." He sat down opposite her at the table. "I want a wife. I want a baby. So far I haven't found anyone I can picture spending the rest of my life with."

"You will," Austin said, squeezing his hand. "You have a lot to offer a woman."

"Not much money."

"That won't matter to the right woman."

"Maybe, maybe not. Do you think I'm being too picky? You know, looking for the perfect person?"

"I think that when you fall in love, that person automatically becomes perfect, or close to it, anyway."

"That's a thought," he said, nodding. "And I think I just heard Dallas's truck pull up. He'll be glad to hear that Scrumptious Sam came through for us."

"Sorry I'm late," Dallas said, coming in the door.

"You look like hell," Houston said. "What's wrong?" Austin turned quickly to look at Dallas. "What happened, brother?"

"I was up all night at the hospital with Joyce. Willie had a really bad asthma attack, and we had to rush him in."

"Oh, that poor baby," Austin said. "Is he all right?"

"He's going to be okay. You should have seen him. He couldn't breathe. He couldn't breathe, Austin. Damn, it was scary. I've never felt so help-less in my life. Look at the size of me, and there wasn't a damn thing I could do."

Houston handed him a cup of coffee. "Sit down, Dallas. You're out on your feet." Dallas slumped onto a chair. "Where are Joyce and Willie now?"

"I took them home, then waited until they were both asleep. I came straight here from Joyce's."

"Well, now *you're* going straight home to bed," Houston said.

"No, I'm ready to work. What's doin'?"

"We got Sam Carter's job," Houston said. "Aus-tin and I can buy supplies. You go home. We'll start the actual work tomorrow."

"Tomorrow is Saturday," Austin said. "I doubt that Sam will want us in his way."

"He said he didn't mind," Houston said. "Even said he'd pay time-and-a-half if we came on the weekend because he's eager to see the place shaped up. So, it's settled. Dallas, go home."

"Yeah, okay," Dallas said, getting to his feet. He walked to the door, then stopped. "The doctors told Joyce that Willie can't live here anymore. She . . . she has to move to Arizona or someplace like that, where Willie will be in a dry, hot climate. They . . . they have to leave soon. I'll see you tomorrow." He hurried out of the door.

"Houston?" Austin said, looking up at him.

"Our Dallas is in a world of hurt, sweetheart. I think he's facing the biggest decision of his life."

Austin got to her feet, her eyes wide. "Do you believe he'll go with Joyce and Willie?"

Houston took a sip of coffee, then nodded. "Could be. I'd say that Dallas Tyler is a man in love, the lucky son of a gun."

"But Arizona?"

"Hey, what can he do? If he does love Joyce and Willie, he'll have to go. He won't have a choice in the matter. He'll tell us when he figures it out."

"But what about Tyler Construction, Houston?"

"I'll worry about that when I need to worry about that."

Austin laughed. "You sound like Mom, except she'd never get around to worrying about it."

" 'Tis true. Okay, short stuff, let's hit the road. We have supplies to get for Scrumptious Sam's house."

The following hours went by quickly. Houston had a specific wholesaler for each different type of material he needed. He had explained early on to Austin that while a company might carry the finest quality paint, their plaster board could be inferior. Many contractors saved time by shopping at one place, but Houston insisted on crisscrossing the area to obtain his supplies. Tyler Construction, he often stated, would eventually have the reputation for excellence that he was striving for. The extra miles and time spent now would pay off later.

But would it? Austin wondered as they drove to yet another warehouse. Would there even be a Tyler Construction if Dallas moved away? She didn't view Dallas's relationship with Joyce as wrong or threatening. She was happy for her brother, would wish him godspeed if, indeed, he had fallen in love with Joyce and her darling Willie.

But facts were facts, Austin mused. There would be drastic changes if Dallas moved away. Houston needed more than a hundred-pound partner who fell through ceilings. Yes, there were many fine, honest construction workers looking for jobs, but Tyler Construction was not in a financial position to pay top wages for a man with superior skills. The Tyler trio paid themselves minimum wage, often postponing payday if need be. Austin had been aware that paychecks were sometimes late, but had thought it was a cash flow problem. She now realized that they were living from job to job, Sam's acceptance of their bid bailing them out of trouble.

Austin had a sick feeling in the pit of her stomach that if Dallas left, Tyler Construction would be a forgotten dream. Houston would have no choice but to hire on with one of the big outfits that were always courting both Houston and Dallas with offers of crew chief positions. Both of her brothers were well known for their honesty and excellence.

But what about her? she thought dismally. She'd worked hard for Tyler Construction, she knew that, but it had been trial and error to discover what she was capable of doing. On a regular crew it would have been error, then fired.

Well, she decided, there was no point in stewing about it now. She'd simply have to wait and see what happened. If Dallas was, indeed, in love with Joyce, that took precedence over everything and everyone.

Love, Austin thought. Being in love. Having that love returned in kind. It must be glorious. She'd seen the beauty of it in her parents' marriage all her life. Dallas could very well have found his special lady, and Houston wished he could discover his.

Love. It was an elusive dream for her. Her brothers played matchmaker at every turn, and she good-naturedly endured their efforts. Their often less-then-wonderful efforts. But she knew in an icy little spot in her heart that she mustn't ever fall in love. To love was to share all and everything, keeping no secrets, hiding no ghosts.

What man, Austin pondered, could handle the truth of her problem, the fact that she was different? No man. It was too much to ask, too overwhelming. A man had his pride, his role, his image to maintain. How could he be expected to deal with the truth about Austin Tyler? He couldn't. No man could. Not even someone as big, and strong, dignified, and intelligent as . . .

"Sam," Houston said.

"What?" Austin yelled, jumping in her seat.

"Did I wake you?"

"I was thinking about something. Houston, we're at Sam's house. Why are we at Sam's house?"

"Because these are his supplies, remember? I said his name because that's his car, apparently, I didn't expect him to be here. A Mercedes. Slick, huh?"

"He's here?" she asked, sitting bolt upright. "Why is he here?"

"Is your record stuck?" Houston turned off the ignition. "The man lives here."

"But he should be at work in the city."

"Guess what?" Houston said dryly. "He didn't go to work today. What is your problem?"

"Nothing," she mumbled, opening the truck door. "Nothing at all."

A crew was busily at work in the front yard. Austin watched them for a moment before walking to the end of the truck, where Houston was leveling a stack of lumber onto his broad shoulder.

"That yard is going to look super," Austin said.

"Yep. The whole place will. I'm glad Sam is here. We can get him to look at color charts for paint. I'm going to go put this stuff on the back porch so it will be covered. Take those color charts inside to Sam."

"Me?" Austin asked, knowing, hearing, and hating the fact that her voice had squeaked.

Houston frowned. "Quit acting so flaky, will ya? Just take the charts to Sam."

"You bet," she said, snatching them up. "I'll do that right now." She didn't move.

"Austin!"

"Oh, jeez," she said, then started toward the house.

At the door, Austin knocked politely and plastered what she hoped was a pleasant, professional smile on her face.

This was no big deal, she told herself. So what if the very sight, the sound, the aroma of Sam Carter melted her bones? So what if she was, at that very moment, reliving the memories of the ecstasy of his kiss and touch? So what if her knees were trembling, and she was a breath away from fainting dead away? So what? She could handle this.

The door was opened.

And Sam was smiling at her.

And Sam was saying, "Hello, Austin" in that sexy voice of his.

And Sam looked scrumptious in faded, tight jeans, and an old Harvard sweatshirt, his dark hair slightly tousled, his blue eyes gazing at her.

Sam.

"Come in, Austin," he said.

"Who?" she asked dazedly. "Oh! Yes, of course," she said, snapping out of her dreamy state. She stepped into the living room. "Well, don't you look spiffy? I somehow didn't picture you as someone who owned faded jeans and a grungy sweatshirt. You really look super-duper."

"You like this, huh?" he said, grinning. "I brought another load of stuff from my apartment. I'd forgotten I even had these clothes. I haven't worn them in years."

"Did you really go to Harvard?"

"Yep. It's a family tradition. All Carter men go to Harvard."

"Oh. What if your son didn't want to go to Harvard? Never mind. That's none of my business."

"My son," Samuel said quietly, "will make his own career decisions. I have no intention of assuming he will be an attorney and attend Harvard Law School. His happiness will be more important than whether or not there are enough Carters at Carter, Carter, and Carter."

"Oh, Sam," Austin whispered, "that's beautiful."

Ah, hell, Samuel thought. Austin had just blown his plan to smithereens. He was supposed to have seen her again when he was well rested and instantly realize she was lovely, but certainly not enough to throw him for a loop.

But there she stood in her jeans and T-shirt, and her cute-as-a-button braids, gazing up at him with her big brown eyes, and he was definitely thrown for a loop. It was, in fact, worse than that. He wanted to haul her into his arms and kiss her. He wanted to mold her soft curves to his hard body, and feel the desire and that indescribable heat weave back and forth between them. A good night's sleep hadn't lessened his attraction to Austin Tyler one iota. If anything, she was more beautiful today than she'd been yesterday.

Now, what in the hell was he going to do?

"Sam?" Austin said. "Is something wrong? You look terribly crabby all of a sudden."

"It's Samuel," he said crossly.

"Well, excuse me," she said. She brushed past him and started across the room.

Samuel spun around and covered the distance between them in two long strides. He gripped her arm, halted her flight, and stepped in front of her.

"I'm sorry," he said, dropping his hand. "I didn't mean to be rude. You can call me Sam. No one else I know calls me Sam and . . . well, I rather like the way it sounds when you say it." He stopped speaking and stared up at the ceiling for a moment before looking at her again. "And," he went on, his voice low and husky, "I like the way you look, and taste, and how you respond to my kisses. I don't know what I'm going to do about you, Austin, but if I don't kiss you in the next three seconds, I'm going to explode. Oh, Lord, now you even have me blithering. I've got to kiss you, Austin. I really do."

She blinked. "Oh. I see. Well. Goodness, then I think that's exactly what you should do, Sam."

He raked a hand through his hair. "I shouldn't. It's not a good idea, because when I kiss you I don't want to stop, then I— Am I really blithering? I've never blithered in my life."

Austin sighed dramatically. "I'm afraid so. Yes, you're definitely blithering. There's only one cure for that." She smiled. "Kiss me again, Sam," she said merrily. "Oh, I've been dying to say that."

He cradled her face in his hands and smiled at

her warmly. "You're wonderful," he said, lowering his head toward hers. "I'll kiss you again, Austin." He brushed his lips over hers. "And again." He gave her a small, nibbling peck. "And again."

"When?" she whispered.

"Right now," he said, and claimed her mouth in a hard, searing kiss.

Austin melted against him, her arms circling his neck as he embraced her to press her close to him. Their tongues met, and passions soared instantly. The kiss was all and more than they remembered. It was want, and need, and a meshing of senses. Glorious.

"Hey, Austin," Houston said, poking his head in the room, "when you get finished there, have Sam look at the color charts."

"Oh, Lord," Sam said, jerking his head up.

" 'Kay," Austin said dreamily. "Color charts."

"Yeah," Houston said, then disappeared.

Sam glanced cautiously over his shoulder, then back at Austin. "Is he always that calm before he breaks someone's kneecaps?"

Austin laughed. "He's not going to break your kneecaps. He likes you, Sam. He wouldn't break your kneecaps even if he didn't like you."

"That's reassuring."

"He might break your nose, but not your kneecaps."

"Oh, Lord."

"But you have nothing to worry about. Both Houston and Dallas think you're A-okay."

"And you? What do you think?"

That she was coming apart at the seams, Austin thought frantically. That she'd nearly burst with joy at the sight of Sam, and nearly wept with relief when he'd kissed her. That something strange and glorious was happening to her, and she was frightened and excited in the same breathless moment. That Sam Carter was evoking heated desire within her, the likes of which she'd never experienced before. And that because of meeting Sam, her life was never going to be the same again. That was what she thought.

"I think you're A-okay too," she said, managing a small smile.

He trailed his thumbs over her cheeks. "Good," he said, smiling.

Their gazes locked. Smiles faded. Heartbeats picked up the thundering rhythm once more as Sam leaned toward Austin and Austin leaned toward Sam.

"Color charts," he murmured.

"Who?" she asked.

"Charts. For colors. Or whatever. I don't know."

"Oh," Austin said, stiffening. "Yes, of course. I'm on duty. I'm a crew member of Tyler Construction. Where did I put them?" She lifted her hand. "Here they are. Color charts." She cleared her throat. "I can't kiss you anymore right now, Sam. I have professional responsibilities here."

"Yes, ma'am," he said, grinning at her. "I understand perfectly. Do I get whatever I want?"

"I beg your pardon?"

"Colors. Are all those shades on those little squares available?"

"Colors," Austin said, nodding. "Go for it," she

said, shoving the cards at him. "They're all labeled. You know, inside paint, outside paint, that sort of thing. We didn't ask you if you liked wallpaper."

"I hate wallpaper. My mother has a different patterned wallpaper in every room in the house. It drives me nuts. Okay," he said, looking at the cards, "let's see here." He wandered over to the sofa and sat down, then glanced back at Austin. "Aren't you coming, Miss Tyler Construction? Shouldn't you be taking notes or something? There are paper and a pencil by the phone there."

"You bet." She snatched up the paper and pencil, then sat ramrod stiff on the edge of the sofa. "I'm ready."

"My bedroom."

She snapped her head around to look at him. "Your bedroom? What about your bedroom?"

"It needs painting."

She looked at the paper again. "Sam's bedroom," she said aloud as she wrote it down. "Check. What color do you want?"

"What do you think would compliment the hole in the ceiling?" he asked, chuckling.

"We're fixing the hole in the ceiling, sir," she said, glaring at him. "What color?"

"Don't rush me," he said, raising his hand. "This is serious business. I have to decide what mood, what aura, atmosphere, I want to create."

"Aura?" Austin said, her eyes widening. "Atmosphere?" Her voice went up an octave. "In your bedroom?"

"Well, sure," he said calmly. "You know, what image I want to evoke. Maybe I'll do it all in red."

"Red?"

Samuel spread his arms across the top of the sofa and squinted at the ceiling. "Yeah. I can see it in my mind. Red satin sheets, furry red bedspread, red walls and ceiling, except for where the mirrors are."

"Mirrors! That's the most disgusting thing I've ever heard."

He looked at her again, all innocence. "It is? I thought it sounded rather . . . unique."

"It sounds like a bordello!"

Samuel fell apart. He hooted with laughter. Austin stared at him with her mouth open. Houston wandered into the room and observed the scene blandly, as though he weren't witnessing anything out of the ordinary. Samuel continued to laugh himself silly.

"Gotcha," he said to Austin, gasping for breath. "You should see your face. I love it, I love it."

Austin jumped to her feet. "Sam Carter, you are not one bit funny. You put a cork in it right this minute. Red bedroom with mirrors, indeed."

"Sounds good to me," Houston said, and shrugged. Austin shot him a stormy look. "I'm kidding!"

"So was I," Samuel said, finally managing to control himself, "but Austin fell for it. A bordello? Oh, man. I didn't think anyone used that word."

"Of course they do," Austin said, sniffing indignantly. "It's been in use since 1598, is of Germanic origin, and is related to the Old English word 'bord,' which was translated into 'brothel.' The French version was—"

"Austin," Houston said, a warning tone to his voice, "we get the point."

" 'Bordel,' " Austin finished lamely. "Forget it," she mumbled, staring at the toe of her tennis shoe. "It's not very interesting, anyway."

"What's interesting," Samuel said, getting to his feet, "is how you knew all that right off the top of your head. That's incredible."

"No, it's boring," Austin said. "If you're quite sure you're done horsing around, we'll get back to business."

"But how did you know all that?' Samuel insisted.

"She . . . um . . . plays a lot of Trivial Pursuit," Houston said quickly. "Ready to go, Austin? I've got everything unloaded."

"Do you have another job to get to?" Sam asked.

"Nope," Houston said. "I have paperwork to plow through this afternoon. We'll be back first thing in the morning to get started here."

"Well, I sure could use some help choosing paint colors. I was thinking that Austin could stay and help me, then I'll drive her home later."

"It's okay with me," Houston said, shrugging again.

"Austin?" Samuel asked.

"Well, I guess so," she said slowly, "if you're certain that you need help."

"Positive," he said, looking directly at her. There it was again, he realized, that strange flicker of sadness in her eyes, a haunted look, close to fear.

She'd rattled off the spiel about the word *bordello*, then a curtain had fallen over her, taking the twinkle from her eyes. Trivial Pursuit? No. No way. There was more to this. It was tied to the episode about the refrigerator and turning off the air conditioner too. And he had every intention of getting to the bottom of it. "I'd like you to stay, Austin."

"All right," she said softly.

"I'll see you tomorrow, then," Houston said, starting toward the door. He opened it, then turned. "Oh, and, Sam?"

"Yes?"

"Take it easy."

The two men exchanged a long look. That hadn't been just a trendy exit line, Samuel realized. Houston, bless him, was warning him to go slow and easy with Austin, knowing he hadn't fallen for the Trivial Pursuit bit.

"Thanks, I will," he said, as Houston left the house.

There was a pressing matter at hand, Sam thought: finding out just who Austin Tyler really is.

Four

For Samuel, the remaining hours of the afternoon were a study in frustration because Austin Tyler was a study in efficiency. She was there to help Sam pick colors of paint for his house, and, by gum, that was what they were going to do.

But now Samuel could detect the clues that meant Austin was tense and upset despite her sunny smile. She talked too fast and continually, and avoided looking directly at him. She declined his offer of going out to dinner with the announcement that she already had plans for the evening. That fact did not sit well with one Mr. Samuel Carter.

The drive to her house was made to the accompaniment of Austin humming along to a tune on the radio while Samuel gritted his teeth. When he pulled into the driveway, having followed Austin's directions, she immediately put her hand on the door of the car.

"I've got to dash," she said. "I'm running late. I think you picked super colors, Sam. 'Bye."

Samuel watched through narrowed eyes as Austin left the car, hurried up the wooden stairs, and disappeared into her apartment. He drummed his fingers on the steering wheel, clenched his jaw even tighter, then backed out of the drive. The words he mumbled as he drove away would have shocked the clients of Carter, Carter, and Carter.

Inside her living room, Austin sank onto the sofa. She'd done it, she thought wearily. She'd escaped. She'd gotten away from Sam without explaining her dissertations on bordellos and refrigerators.

Now, she realized, the evening stretched interminably before her. She didn't have other plans, she'd had plans only *not* to be cornered by Sam Carter.

He knew, she thought dismally. He knew there was something different about her. What she shared with Sam was temporary, she knew that, but she didn't want it tarnished by the truth. She wanted Sam to see her as a beautiful woman. A woman he pulled into his arms and kissed, held, touched. A woman who ignited his passion just as he did hers.

A restlessness seized Austin, and the walls of her small apartment seemed to be closing in on her. She stepped outside and saw her father unloading groceries from the car. Teddy Tyler was, indeed, bigger than his two burly sons, and just as gentle. He was a retired mailman, and spent his time tending to the Tyler home and fishing.

"Hi, Dad," Austin called, then ran down the stairs to where he stood by the trunk of the car.

"Hello, Austin," Teddy said, beaming at her. "How's my favorite daughter?"

"I'm your only daughter," she said. She smiled as she completed their greeting that had become a long-standing ritual. She picked up a bag of groceries. "Is Mom home?"

"Nope. She's at a garden club affair of some sort. Come inside and talk to me while I put this food away."

The pair entered the cheerful blue and white kitchen, and Austin began to help unload the food from the bags. When every item had been put away, and Teddy had handed Austin a tall glass of iced tea without either of them having spoken, he waved her onto a chair at the kitchen table, then sat opposite her.

"This is where we always came with our problems," Austin said quietly, "to you, here at this table."

"And we solved them," her father said. "Together. You're my second customer of the day. Dallas has sat in that chair already, looking like you, eyes as sad as a basset hound's."

"Dallas is facing a very big decision."

"That he is," Teddy said, nodding. "He'll make the right one. My children always do."

"Dad, have you ever minded that it always had to be you at this table instead of Mom?"

"Lordy, no. I wouldn't change one thing about your mother. I love that woman just as she is. Always have, always will. I know she'd just pat you on the head and tell you not to worry about whatever it is that has you troubled. Bless her heart, she's wonderful. But you, Dallas, and Houston know that life's problems can't always be handled your mother's way. So, my darling girl, talk to your old dad. What's his name?"

"Who?"

"The fella who has you looking like a sad-eyed basset hound."

"I never indicated that a man was involved in what I wanted to discuss with you."

"Austin, this is your father you're speaking to."

"Sam." She sighed. "His name is Sam. Samuel Carter of Carter, Carter, and Carter, Attorneys-at-Law. Scrumptious Sam."

Teddy laughed. "Scrumptious, is he? I like that word." He became serious again. "Okay, let me guess. You've decided that there's no hope for you and Scrumptious Sam because of what you believe to be your problem, the fact that you're different."

"Yes. I've slipped up a couple of times, and he's getting curious. I'm usually so careful, but I relaxed with Sam, and flubbed."

"Oh, Austin, I blame myself for all of this. I should never have let you go to that institute. I was convinced it was the best thing for you, and it was so terribly wrong."

"It wasn't your fault. It's no one's fault that I am like I am."

"Sweetheart, I've run out of ways to try to convince you that you have a rare and wonderful gift. You can't run from this any longer. You are—"

"No," Austin interrupted. "Don't say it. I don't want to hear that word."

Teddy gripped her hands. "Yes. I'm going to say it. We've edged around it for too many years because it upset you. I blame the people at the institute for that, for not treating you with a human touch. But that's all behind you now. You are a genius! You are one of the most intelligent people in this country!"

"No!" she said, trying to free her hands as tears filled her eyes.

"Yes!" he said, refusing to let her go. He stood and pulled her to her feet, wrapping his huge arms around her slender body. "Yes, my darling girl. Cry if you want to. But, Austin? It's time to stop running. I can't stand by and watch this anymore. You've been back with us for nearly four years, and you're still running. No more. No more, do you hear me?"

"Oh, Daddy," she said, sobbing into his shirt. "I don't know what to do with my life. I don't know who I am. And now there's Sam, and he's so wonderful, but I'm so afraid that if he knew, it would be like it's always been. I'm a freak! He'd never want to see me again because he wouldn't know what to do or say around me." She choked on a sob. "I went on and on about the bordello, Daddy. He knows. He knows there's something weird about me."

"Hush now," he said, rubbing her back. "You'll get the hiccups."

"And the institute wrote me a letter and—"

"What?" Teddy asked, stiffening.

"I didn't read it, but I know what they want. I won't go back there. Not ever."

"Damn right, you won't. You leave them to me and Houston. Dallas has enough on his mind. The institute won't bother you again. Now, sit back down at the table." He pulled a handkerchief out of his pocket. "Blow your nose."

Austin did as instructed, feeling all of four years old but not caring. She blew her nose, took a wobbly breath, and looked at her father.

"That's better," he said. "Now, tell me about Sam."

"We're remodeling his house. Oh, Dad, he's beautiful. I met him when I fell through the ceiling, and he was only wearing underwear, and he's just so scrumptious. When he . . . I've never felt . . . And then when he . . . oh, it's heaven."

"I think I'll pass on the ceiling and the underwear. If you're remodeling his house, then Dallas and Houston have met him, right?"

"Oh, yes," she said quickly, "and they really like him."

"Good. That covers that part, at least. Darling girl, listen to me. You've got that special glow about you, that look in your eyes when you speak of Sam. I've never seen you like this. You deserve the chance to discover what you and Sam might have together."

"But . . ."

"No. Tell him, Austin. Tell him you're a genius."

"You don't understand. A man can't accept—"

"Ah," Teddy interrupted again, "there's the key word . . . man. A real man, a man worthy of my darling Austin, won't have a minute's trouble with the fact that you're a smart cookie. If Sam Carter is intimidated by your intelligence, he's not worth having, I don't care how beautiful he looks in his underwear. Does Houston know about the underwear scene?"

"Yes."

"Then it can't be as bad as it sounds, or Sam would have a broken nose. *Austin, tell Sam Carter.*"

"I'll—I'll think about it."

"Well, that's a start. Just remember that the longer you postpone it, the harder it will be. Do it, Austin. For yourself. For Sam."

Austin got up and went to the other side of the table to throw her arms around her father's neck. "Thank you, Daddy. I love you so much."

"I love you too, darling girl. You'll do what's right, just as Dallas will."

"I'll talk to you soon," she said, then hurried out the back door.

Teddy watched her go, then got to his feet. He went to the wall phone and punched in a number.

"Houston? I know you're working tomorrow, but on Sunday you and I are taking a little trip. The institute is bothering Austin again. We're going to put an end to it, once and for all. . . . Yes, it will be my pleasure too. I'll make the plane reservations and let you know what time I'll pick you up. Oh, and, Houston? Be prepared to fill me in completely on Sam Carter."

. . . .

Saturday morning found Sam in a lousy mood. He hadn't slept well. He had tossed and turned, then had disturbing dreams that made no sense when he finally dozed.

Austin Tyler had haunted him through the long, dark night.

Sam stood by the front window, sipping a cup of coffee, looking out over his now neat-as-a-pin yard, and fuming. Since waking at dawn, his thoughts had resembled Ping-Pong balls. Back and forth, back and forth they'd gone. He never wanted to see Austin again; he checked the clock every few minutes, wondering when she and her brothers would arrive.

He glanced down at his faded jeans and very faded Harvard T-shirt, and shook his head. Austin liked him in what she called his "grungy clothes," and he'd dressed with the idea of pleasing her.

He moaned, looking up at the ceiling. "I can't stand it." He was going to change into slacks and a dress shirt, and quit acting like a jerk trying to impress the head cheerleader. Yes, he was going to go change. No, he wasn't. And he knew it. "Ah, hell."

Sam stiffened, every nerve ending in his body seeming to come alive as a truck pulled into the driveway. A truck containing Dallas and Houston, but no Austin.

No Austin? his mind roared. Where was she? Was she sick? Had she decided not to see him again? How dare she decide not to see him again!

She couldn't do that. He wouldn't stand for it. But what if she were sick? How sick? Oh, Lord.

Samuel set his mug on a table and strode to the front door, flinging it open. He just barely missed receiving Houston's knuckles in his nose, as Houston had been prepared to knock on the door.

"Where is she?" Samuel shouted, not bothering with a polite greeting.

"She?" Houston said, all innocence. "She who?"

"Don't mess with me, Tyler," Sam said, almost growling. "I'm not in the mood."

"She," Houston said, grinning at him, "is at the paint store. She'll be along in a bit. May we come in?"

"Certainly," Sam said, throwing up his hands. "Now that I've made a complete idiot of myself, come on in. Are you Houston or Dallas?"

"Houston. The inferior clone behind me is Dallas," Houston said, stepping into the house. Dallas followed him. "You're a bit uptight this morning, Sam."

"Women," Dallas said with a snort of disgust. "They'll do it to you every time. Your life is in order, then bam, you're a dead duck. Women should be banned from the face of the earth."

"That," Houston said, rolling his eyes to the heavens, "was the dumbest thing you've ever said in your entire life."

"You're right," Dallas said miserably. "Ignore me. I'm a wreck. A basket case."

"So is Sam," Houston said, jerking his head in Sam's direction.

"I am not," Sam said indignantly. "I was merely concerned about Austin's health, that's all."

"Oh, okay," Houston said, chuckling. "If I buy that, I suppose that next up is some swampland you want to sell me to build condos on. Well, this ought to be an all-time fun day. I'm in the company of gloom and doom. Come on, sunshine face," he said to Dallas. "Let's get the new baseboards on so Austin can paint them. You know Austin, Sam. Our sister? The cute little gal who's at the paint store?"

"Can it, Tyler," Sam said, glaring at him. Houston hooted.

"Your day will come, Houston," Dallas said as the brothers crossed the room. "You're going to fall in love and fall apart. And I'm going to laugh myself blue."

Love? Sam thought. Oh, now, wait just a minute here. Dallas Tyler might be tied up in knots over a woman because he was in love with her, but Samuel Carter certainly wasn't in love with Austin Tyler. That was ridiculous, totally absurd.

No, Sam reaffirmed in his mind, he wasn't in love. He was intrigued by Austin. She was different from any woman he'd ever known, breath of fresh air compared to the glitzy, sophisticated women he saw socially. Austin said whatever was on her mind with a refreshing honesty. Granted, some of the topics sent his libido into overdrive, but it was still a nice change. She was unusual, too, in that she seemed unaware of her own beauty, didn't flaunt it.

And she had the only eyes he'd ever seen that actually twinkled.

So, he did feel rather protective toward her when

she would suddenly become so sad. He had the urge to hold her close, shield her from whatever was upsetting her and taking the sparkle, the twinkle, from her eyes. There was a vulnerability about Austin that brought out his masculine instincts to beat the wolves from the door and keep her from harm.

And, he thought dryly, a few other of his masculine instincts were also ready and willing for action. Lord, how he wanted to make love to that woman.

But that didn't mean he was in love with her!

Fine, he thought decisively. He'd figured out that there were many facets to his dilemma. He would simply approach them as separate entities as he would clauses of a complicated contract. Each would be unraveled, solved, his control regained. Step by step he would take charge of himself again, then bid Austin Tyler adieu.

And he would be alone.

Samuel blinked as the realization of that last thought landed with a painful thud in the pit of his stomach.

He pressed the heels of his hands to his now throbbing temples, and shook his head. He was going insane, he thought with alarming calmness. It was a rotten shame, but he was slipping right over the edge. They'd cart him away, clicking their tongues in sympathy, and that would be the last of Samuel Carter.

And it was all Austin Tyler's fault!

Had he asked for her to come flying through his ceiling? No, he had not. Was it fair that she was so damn beautiful, had hair like an auburn waterfall, was laughing one minute, sad the next? No, it was not. Did it make sense that kisses shared with a fragile little creature with an aura of vulnerability and innocence about her could turn him inside out, aching for more? No, it did not!

And, therefore, the deteriorating state of his mind and body was entirely Austin's fault.

And he could cheerfully wring her neck!

The sound of a vehicle pulling into the driveway pulled Sam from his jumbled thoughts, and he strode to the window to look out.

Austin.

She slipped off the seat of the truck, flipped a single braid to her back, and closed the truck door.

Sam's heart thundered in his chest.

Austin started toward the house.

Go away! Sam's mind yelled in near panic.

Hurry, Austin, his heart whispered.

Sam jerked as a light knock sounded at the door. At the same moment that his brain was demanding that he hightail it upstairs to his room to hide, his feet were carrying him to the door. His hand lifted and opened the door. His arms enfolded Austin into his embrace, he hauled her inside, and his lips came down hard on hers.

Austin's eyes widened in shock at the unexpected greeting, then an instant later her lashes drifted down as she parted her lips to receive Sam's questing tongue into her mouth. As she splayed her hands on his back, she could feel the tension in his muscles, was aware of the coiled tightness of his entire body. The kiss was rough, frenzied, and she knew, even as desire churned within her, that something was wrong.

Sam lifted his head to draw a ragged breath, but before he could take possession of her mouth again, Austin looked directly into his eyes. She saw the smoky hue that radiated the message of his desire for her.

"Sam?" she asked breathlessly. "What's wrong?"

He cleared his throat, then stepped back. "Wrong?" He reached behind her and closed the door, wondering absently if the neighbors had enjoyed the little show just performed in the doorway. "What makes you think there's something wrong?"

"You didn't say hello."

"Oh. Hello, Austin. How are you today?" He smiled at her rather weakly.

"Fine," she said, squinting at him. "Are you all right?"

"As all right as any insane person can be, I suppose."

"What?"

"Cut the hanky-panky," Dallas called. "I'm coming through."

"Oh, for crying out loud," Sam said.

Dallas came into the room with long, thin boards wobbling on top of one of his broad shoulders. "Baseboards are ready for paint in the kitchen, Austin. Houston is unloading the truck. I'll get started in here."

"Okay," she said. "How is Willie, Dallas?"

Dallas leveled the wood off of his shoulder and onto the floor. "He's still worn out. It was a bad attack. Joyce gave her two-week notice at work."

"She's leaving in two weeks?" Austin said, her eyes widening.

"Yeah. Working for a big insurance company with offices all over the country has advantages, especially since her boss here really appreciates how hard she works. He got on the phone to see what jobs were open at other branches. She has a position waiting for her in Tucson."

"Tucson, Arizona," Austin said. "Oh, my, that's so far away."

"Yeah, tell me about it," Dallas said sullenly. "Go paint."

"Right," Austin said. She glanced quickly at Sam, then hurried toward the kitchen.

"Your . . . um . . . lady is moving to Tucson, Dallas?" Sam asked.

"She has to. Her son, Willie, has asthma. The doctors said he has to get out of this climate."

"That makes sense. But what about you? What are you going to do?"

"Sam, my mind is mush. I keep going over it, and over it, pro and con. Do you realize that if I go, that would be the end of Tyler Construction? Houston couldn't afford to get the kind of guy he'd want to take my place. That would leave Austin high and dry, and that's a rotten thing to do to her because she doesn't feel comfortable around people she doesn't know. As hard as she tries at other jobs, it just never seems to work out. But the thought of Joyce and Willie going off without me blows my mind."

"You really love this Joyce, don't you?"

"Yeah."

"I think that both Austin and Houston would say that your love for Joyce comes first."

"That's what my dad said. I don't know. I need more time to sort it all through."

Sam nodded, then leaned his shoulder against the wall as he watched Dallas begin to pry off the old baseboards.

"Dallas," he said finally, "why does Austin have such a rough time at other jobs? Why would she feel uncomfortable around strangers?"

"It's complicated, Sam, and it's not my place to explain it to you. Austin will tell you if she wants you to know about her problem."

"Problem?"

"Her word, not mine. That's how she sees it. She feels she's different, has this—I've said enough. Don't push her about it, Sam. She needs a lot of space when it comes to this thing."

"What thing?"

"I can't tell you."

"Damn."

"Sam?" Dallas said.

"Yes?"

"Don't hurt her. Houston and I like you . . . so far. I imagine you're used to sophisticated, worldly women, who know how to play the game. Austin isn't like that."

"I know, Dallas."

"Yeah, well, it's a lot more involved than her just living a sheltered life. You seem sincerely interested in her, but if you're not, if you're just killing time, then back off. Houston and I won't stand by and watch her get hurt."

"I understand."

"I hope you do."

"Are you threatening me, Dallas?"

"Yep."

"I thought you were," Samuel said, nodding.

"So far, you're okay."

"I appreciate that. She's driving me nuts, you know. Right out of my ever-lovin' mind."

Dallas chuckled. "Join the club, chum. The power that hundred-pound women have over two-hundred-pound men is amazing. I think my brain is dissolving."

"Ditto."

"Good luck, Sam."

"Same to you, Dallas," he said, then wandered slowly in the direction of the kitchen.

Austin had a problem? he wondered. Something that made her feel different from other people? Like what? Some kind of learning disability? Dyslexia, perhaps? Or maybe she couldn't retain instructions long enough to carry them out properly. No, that didn't wash. There was nothing wrong with Austin's memory, as evidenced by the sermonette on the bordello.

She obviously wasn't physically impaired, he mused, so it had to be her mind, brain, something to do with her thinking processes. She was a lousy speller? Hell, so was he. No, it was tied into the bordello and the refrigerator, he was sure of it. And he didn't have the foggiest notion as to what her mysterious problem was. What he did know was that it made her very, very sad, and he wanted to fix it for her right now.

Despite the turmoil in Samuel's mind, a smile lit up his face when he entered the kitchen and viewed the scene before him. Austin was on her hands and knees on newspapers, concentrating on painting the baseboards. Her bottom was poked up in the air, and Sam had to restrain himself from giving it a friendly pat. Her jean-clad bottom also boasted a stripe of pale yellow paint. She had twisted her braid onto the top of her head to keep it, Sam surmised, out of the paint bucket.

She looked, he decided, adorable.

He pulled a chair from the table and flipped it around, straddling it as he crossed his arms over the top of the back.

"Having fun?" he asked.

"Actually, the blood is rushing to my head, but if I don't pass out cold, I'm all set. I always get stuck with this job."

"You have paint on your cute tush."

"I know. I slipped and sort of slid into the lid there on the floor. Oh, well." She paused. "Do you really think I have a cute tush?"

"I certainly do."

She laughed. "That's nice."

"I wish you'd look at me. It's a bit disconcerting talking to said cute tush, Austin."

"Can't. I have to keep at this. Are you going to tell me what was wrong with you when I first arrived?"

Sam pulled his gaze from her yellow-striped bottom. "No. Not right now."

"Okay."

"You gave up awfully easily."

"I respect people's rights to have private thoughts."

"And secrets?"

"That depends."

"On what?"

"Well, Sam, it depends on the relationship. Secrets between lovers, people in love, can be dangerous in my opinion. But in every kind of relationship, there's room for private thoughts. Make sense?"

"Yes." He watched as she scooted farther along the floor. "Try this one on for size. Don't you think there are some secrets that should be brought into the open *before* people become lovers, and are in a position where they might fall in love?"

Austin's hand holding the paintbrush trembled slightly, then she steadied it. "Yes," she said softly, "there are secrets like that."

"Austin," he said gently, "look at me for just a minute."

"But I have to get this painting—"

"Please."

Austin sighed and set the brush on the edge of the can of paint. She turned to sit Indian-style on the floor, stared at the baseboard for a long moment, then slowly met Sam's gaze.

Oh, dear heaven, his mind raced, she looked so frightened, so fragile, as if she were about to splinter into a million pieces. Should he back off? Leave her alone? No, he couldn't. He just couldn't.

Had he meant what he said? Did he see *himself* as someone who might be falling in love? Hell, he didn't know. All he knew right now was that he hated this secret that stood between them, hated the sadness it brought to Austin's beautiful, big brown eyes.

"You know, don't you?" she said, her voice not quite steady.

"I know there's something troubling you, something you're keeping from me. I'd like to help, if you'd give me a chance."

"There's nothing that you or anyone can do. Facts are facts." She took a deep, wobbly breath. "I'm different from other people, Sam."

"Okay. It's not physical, is it?"

"No."

"Austin, this is obviously very difficult for you to discuss, so I'll just put it out on the table. Do you have a learning disability of some kind?"

Her eyes widened. "Is *that* what you think?"

"What I think is that if you do, it doesn't matter because there are ways of working around these things. You're proving that right now by being a part, an important part, of Tyler Construction. Ah, damn, Austin, I can't stand it. I can't bear to see the sadness in your eyes whenever you think about whatever this thing is. I'm here, I'll help you find a solution, I swear it."

"Oh, Sam," she whispered, her eyes misting with tears, "thank you. That means more to me than I can ever tell you. But, Sam, you've got it all wrong, backward. I don't have a learning disability."

"You don't?"

"No."

"Then what—"

"I—I'm a . . . I'm a genius. I'm one of the most intelligent"—tears spilled onto her cheeks—"people in this country. I'm sorry, Sam. For you, for me." She choked on a sob.

Samuel stiffened in the chair, staring at Austin with a stunned expression on his face.

"Oh, no," she sobbed, stumbling to her feet. "Oh, God, please don't look at me like that, like I'm a freak, like . . . oh, please." She ran out the back door.

"Dear Lord, what have I done?" Sam mumbled. He was up and moving, barreling out the door after Austin.

He collided with the brick wall of Houston Tyler's body. Houston Tyler, who had his arms crossed over his massive chest, and who was glowering at Samuel Carter. Houston Tyler, who was definitely not a happy man.

Five

"You've got some explaining to do, Carter," Houston said. "What did you say to Austin?"

"Dammit, man, move your carcass! I've got to go after her."

"You're not going near her," Houston said, his voice rising. "You made her cry. What did you say to her?"

"Nothing! That's what's wrong. She told me, Houston. She told me that she's a genius, and I was so stunned, I just—"

"Stared at her," he interrupted, shaking his head, "like she was a freak. You blew it, Sam."

"I had it all figured out that she had some kind of learning disability," Sam said none too softly. "I told her that I'd help her any way I could, then she announced that she was a genius. Of course I was shocked. That possibility was the furthest thing from my mind."

"And now?" Houston said, not budging. "How do you feel about it?"

"Feel? What's to feel? Austin is a genius. Fine. Dandy. I sure as hell don't see it as the problem she views it as. My God, she was apologizing to me for it. That's nuts. Who did this to her? Who made her feel like a freak?"

"That's a long, grim story."

"Which I don't have time for at the moment. Listen, you human mountain, I'm going to talk to Austin right now. I'm going to make her understand that she is the most beautiful, most wonderful, the most—Houston, you have three seconds to get out of my way, or I swear to heaven I'm going to take you apart. You'll probably break my face in the process, but I'm going to go through, over, or around you. Austin needs me."

Houston's deep scowl slowly changed into a smile, then to a wide grin. He stepped back with a sweep of his arm.

"Go for it," he said. "Let it not be said that Houston Tyler stood in the way of true love."

"I never said I was in love. . . . Oh, forget it. Where is she?"

"Behind that apple tree in the back of the yard. Sam?"

"Yeah?"

"I'm trusting you with her."

"I hear you," Sam said quietly. "I never meant to make her cry. I can't handle it when she's sad. I'll make her smile again, Houston. Somehow."

"I hope so," he said, concern evident in his voice. "Austin has had a rough time of it. As much as we all love her, even as big as we are, there are things we can't protect her from. Be careful, Sam. She's so damn fragile."

"I know. Thanks, Houston," he said, then took off at a run across the yard.

"Love sure is something to behold," Houston said to no one. He turned and walked slowly into the house.

The fact that the backyard had been perfectly manicured by the landscaping crew he'd hired went unnoticed by Sam as he ran toward the apple tree. He slowed his pace, tried to collect his racing thoughts, then mentally threw up his hands in defeat.

He did not, he realized, stopping in his tracks, have the foggiest idea what to say to a weeping Austin. If she were a contract with a clause out of whack, he'd know exactly what to do to rectify and gain control of the situation. But she was a woman. A crying woman. A sad, terribly upset woman.

She was also a genius.

A genius, he repeated in his mind. Austin? Austin, who fell through ceilings and told him he was scrumptious? Austin, who looked like a dream, kissed like a dream, even cooked like a dream, was a genius?

Despite his bold statement to Houston that it presented no problem, Sam suddenly realized that he'd never met a real live honest-to-goodness genius before. How did an ordinary man—well, not

Get one full-length Loveswept FREE every month!
Now you can be sure you'll never, ever miss a single
Loveswept title by enrolling in our special reader's home
delivery service. A service that will bring you all six new
Loveswept romances each month for the price of five—and
deliver them to you before they appear in the bookstores!

Examine 6 Loveswept Novels for

15 days FREE!

(SEE OTHER SIDE FOR DETAILS)

totally ordinary. He *had* graduated at the top of his class in college. Still, what did a contract lawyer say to a genius without coming across as an idiot?

Now, wait just a minute here, Sam thought. He hadn't had any difficulty talking to Austin *before* he knew how intelligent she was. He hadn't had any problem deciding she was the most refreshing, delightful, desirable woman he'd ever met.

Austin Tyler was the only woman he had ever loved.

"Oh, my Lord," Sam whispered.

He loved her.

He was in love with Austin.

And she was a genius?

"Oh, my Lord," he whispered again.

Sam shook his head and walked the remaining distance to the enormous old apple tree. He peered around it and felt a sharp pain in his chest. Austin had her arms wrapped around drawn-up knees, her head was bent, and she was crying softly. He pulled a handkerchief from his pocket, went to her side, and set the handkerchief on her knees.

"Austin, may I sit down?" he asked quietly.

She snatched up the handkerchief and dabbed at her nose without looking at him. "No."

"Thank you. You're most kind." He lowered himself to the ground beside her, leaned back against the tree trunk, and stretched his legs out in front of him.

"Go away, Sam," she said, then hiccuped.

"I can't do that. I have to talk to you."

"No."

"Okay. I'll talk out loud to myself, and maybe you'll catch a word or two. It's perfectly understandable that I would talk to myself, because I'm a nut case. You, Austin Tyler, have driven me right out of my mind. I'm certifiably insane."

Austin's head popped up. "That's the most ridiculous thing I've ever heard," she said, looking at him. "You know where you're going, who you are. You're not a cuckoo."

He turned his head slowly to look at her, a tightness gripping his throat as he saw her tear-stained face. He forced himself to adopt what he hoped was a bland expression on his face. He gripped his thighs with his hands to keep from hauling Austin into his arms.

"Oh?" he said. "Is that so? Well, you're wrong. I'm completely out of control. My control is kaput, zapped, zinged."

"Zinged?"

"Definitely zinged. Gone. Vanished. You did that to me, Austin."

"Me?" she said, her eyes widening.

"You," he said, nodding solemnly. "From the moment you fell through the ceiling, I totally lost it." He sighed dramatically.

"Well, find it! You can't go around zinged and zapped just because someone fell through your ceiling. You have important things to do with your life."

"And so," he said gently, "do you."

Austin stared at him for a long moment, then shook her head. "No. No, I don't. You don't understand. You just don't understand." Her voice quivered and there was a frantic edge to it as tears filled her eyes once more. "Go away. Leave me alone. Please, Sam, just leave me be. I saw your face when I told you that I was a genius. I saw the way you looked at me."

"Well, dammit," he said, his voice rising, "what did you expect? I'd tried to figure out what made you become so sad for no apparent reason. It was like putting a puzzle together. I came up with the wrong conclusion, and thought you had a learning disability. When you said you were a genius, I was stunned because I'd been so off the track. You didn't even give me a chance to comment. You decided how I felt about it. That was very rude."

"Rude? Me? You're the one who looked at me as though I were a freak."

"No. *You* decided I looked at you oddly. Yes, I was surprised, and I suppose that showed on my face, but I don't think you're a freak. You happen to be a genius. So? What do you want me to do? Kiss your foot? Bow three times? Ask you to predict what the stock market is going to do? So, you're smart. Well, I'm still taller than you are, stronger than you are, I'm allowed in men's rest rooms, and you're not." He shrugged. "It all evens out in the end."

Austin eyed him warily. "You're right. You're crazy."

He waved a hand breezily in the air. "That has already been established. We'll just have to work around that."

Austin sighed, leaned her head back against

the tree, and closed her eyes. "Oh, Sam, you just don't understand. My being a genius is a tremendous problem, a liability."

"Worse than your not being allowed in men's rooms?" He picked up her hand and placed it on his thigh, covering it with his own. "Ah, Austin, I guess I *don't* understand. I've heard you say that you're looking for your place, where you fit in. Yet, I'd think you could be anything you wanted to be, go anywhere you wanted to go. What happened? Where did you get the idea that you were a freak? Talk to me. Help me understand."

"Why?" she asked, not opening her eyes.

Because he loved her, Sam thought. It was as simple and as complicated as that. He was in love with her. But this wasn't the time to tell her. "Why should you talk to me, help me understand?" he asked. "Because something very special is happening between us, Austin. I feel it when you walk into the room. I feel it when I kiss and hold you. I feel it when I merely think about you."

Austin opened her eyes and looked at him, her bottom lip trembling. "Ohhh, that's so sweet."

"Do *you* feel it?" he said, his voice low. He looked directly into her eyes. "Do you, Austin?"

"Yes," she whispered, "but I don't know what it is."

For a genius, she sure was dumb sometimes, he thought. It was love! "We'll worry about what it is later. The fact that you realize that something is happening between us is enough for now. Talk to me, Austin. Who made you feel like a freak?"

"The people—" She dashed the tears from her

cheeks with one hand, but made no attempt to free the hand trapped by Sam's on his thigh. "The people at the institute."

"What institute?" he prodded gently.

"It's a big white building in the middle of nowhere. It wasn't my father's fault. He thought it would be challenging for me because I was bored, restless."

"Wait. Where is this institute? Near here?"

"It's in New York. Up state."

"Oh, okay. And your father sent you there?"

"Yes. Sam, I had graduated from high school when I was twelve, had two bachelor degrees and a master's by the time I was seventeen. I really didn't have any friends because I was so much younger than everyone at college. But it didn't bother me, because I lived at home, and my parents treated me as though I were normal. My father taught me how to cook, my mother played Chutes and Ladders with me when I was little, Houston and Dallas taught me how to ride a bike. No one paid much attention to my intelligence."

"I see. You have a terrific family. You really do."

"I know, and I love them all so much. Anyway, when I was seventeen I got bored with college, but my parents didn't feel I was emotionally mature enough to work for the type of company that could utilize my knowledge. I studied on my own for a while, wrote technical articles for engineering and computer journals, just filling my days with this and that. When I was eighteen my father heard about the institute."

"And?"

"Oh, it's highly recommended, has a top-notch reputation for working with the gifted, with geniuses. My father, Houston, and Dallas went to see it. They listened to the director, heard about all the things that would challenge me, help me use the potential of my mind. My father decided it wouldn't be fair to keep all those advantages from me."

"So you went?"

"Yes. On the surface it was wonderful. I mean, I wasn't different, I fit in, I wasn't the youngest. But, Sam? They never heard of Chutes and Ladders, or learning to cook, or riding a bike. They didn't understand why I was homesick and missed my family. I wasn't a person there, I was a brain that happened to be in a human body. It was so sterile, and white, and no one laughed."

"Oh, Austin," he said, squeezing her hand.

"I'd come home for the holidays and tell everyone that it was great at the institute. I was trying so hard to fit in. I felt like a freak, like a bug under a microscope. They were watching me, always watching me. Everyone else seemed to love it there, but I was so unhappy."

"How long were you there?"

"Two years."

Sam shook his head.

"Houston decided to surprise me with a visit. The director welcomed him in, then took him to a room where he could watch me through a special mirrored wall that I couldn't see through. I was working on a computer program, writing it, in this big white room. The director beamed at Houston and said, 'Our little Fourteen twenty-two is doing beautifully. You should be very proud of her.' "

"Fourteen twenty-two?"

"That was me. I was a number. Not once in those two years did anyone call me Austin."

"Dear God," Sam whispered, feeling the anger building within him.

"They said it was easier that way because our work was logged on a computer and . . . I don't know."

"What did Houston say?"

"Say? Not much." She chuckled. "He just barged into that white room and said that he was taking me home. The director was shouting, trying to stop him, but—"

"Let me guess," Sam said. "Houston broke the guy's nose."

"Yes. Oh, Sam, I was so glad to be home. I didn't want to think about the fact that I was a genius, not ever, ever again. It took me months to relax, realize I was really safely back with my family. I kept waiting for them to come for me, make me return to the institute, to being a number, a freak. My father was ridden with guilt, but it wasn't his fault. All the other geniuses at the institute loved it, they really did."

"It's over, Austin. It's all in the past."

"I know, but I've never forgotten what it was like. I was determined that no one would ever find out how smart I was. My degrees were highly technical, so I took jobs as a secretary, a waitress, a clerk in a store, all kinds of things. But at every single job I slipped up. I'd see ways to cut costs, run things more efficiently. I got on people's nerves and they'd fire me. I just didn't fit in anywhere."

"So you went to work for your brothers."

She sighed. "They've been wonderful to me, but I have to face the fact that I'm only draining their finances and not really helping much."

"Oh, I don't know," he said, smiling. "You fall through ceilings very well."

"And met you," she said softly. "Scrumptious Sam. All I was asking for was a little time with you because you made me feel so special, so beautiful, so womanly. But I went on about the refrigerator and the bordello. I ruined everything."

"No, you didn't."

"Yes, I did. Now you know all about me. You've already wondered how to talk to me, haven't you? Wondered what to say to a genius?"

"Well, I—"

"It's not your fault. It's a very natural reaction. I'm sorry, Sam. I wish I were different, but I can't change what's in my head. What you and I shared was wonderful, and I'll cherish those memories."

"What are you saying?"

"I won't see you after today."

"The hell you won't."

"It won't work, Sam. Believe me, I know. This will stand between us like a wall. You'll weigh and measure what you say, you'll start to watch me. You won't comment on the weather because you'll wonder if geniuses deal in the mundane. Oh, Sam, don't you see? What was happening between us was so warm, but it will turn cold."

"No!" He gripped her upper arms. "No, it won't be like that, Austin. Don't do this to us. Give us a chance. You're quitting, throwing us away."

"I have no choice!"

He couldn't lose her, he thought frantically. He loved her! He needed her to make his life complete, to fill the void he hadn't even realized was there until he'd met her. And he wanted her. He wanted to make love with her, experience for the first time the beautiful difference between having sex and making love with a woman he loved. He wanted to plant his seed deep within her and watch her grow big with his child. He'd love, protect, and cherish Austin Tyler for the remainder of his days. But he couldn't do any of that if she left him.

"I'm so sorry, Sam," Austin said, fresh tears misting her eyes.

"I'm not letting you go," he said fiercely, then brought his mouth down hard onto hers.

The kiss was too rough, but Austin didn't care. He was gripping her arms too tightly, but Austin didn't care. Sobs were catching in her throat, but Austin didn't care.

Because this was Sam.

And then the kiss gentled. Tongues met and dueled. Sam gathered Austin into the warm circle of his arms and held her, making her feel as though she were made of the most delicate china. Making her feel special, and beautiful, and so wanted.

She didn't want to leave him, she thought hazily. Not Sam. Not her Scrumptious Sam. She wanted to spend the rest of her life seeing his smile, hearing his voice, reaching out for him and saying, "Kiss me again, Sam."

Was she, she wondered foggily, in love with Sam Carter? She didn't know. It didn't matter. She had to leave him. She couldn't bear to stay and watch the changes come over him, see him looking at her and trying to decide what to say, how to behave around her. And it would happen. She'd seen it in the past when she'd been open and candid about being a genius, before she'd gone to the institute. She'd seen the shock, the backing away. She couldn't bear to watch the changes in Sam.

Tears spilled onto Austin's cheeks, and Samuel lifted his head. "Did I hurt you, Austin? I'm sorry. I was too rough at first, but I couldn't stand the thought of losing you."

"No, you didn't hurt me."

"I can't let you go, Austin," he said, his voice gritty. "Don't you see that? Don't you see that we deserve a chance?" Didn't she love him even a little bit? Didn't she? He knew she felt something very special when they were together. He *knew* she did. "Austin, are you listening to me?"

She moved slowly out of his embrace and looked up at him. Looked at him, Samuel decided as his heart beat wildly, with the saddest eyes he'd ever seen. Big and brown and glistening with tears, the sight of Austin's eyes seemed to tear him to shreds.

"I hear you, Sam," she said softly, "but it's hopeless. I can't lose the memories of you too. I want to keep *something* from what we've shared."

"Austin, please—"

"No," she interrupted, "now *you* must listen to *me*. I know you believe that my being a genius isn't going to make a difference between us, but it is. I saw it happen too many times before I went to the institute."

"*Before* you went? You were only a child then, it was years ago. This is now, this is me. Is it fair to judge me on the performance of people in your past? What gives you the right to lump me into a group of which I had no part?" He was grabbing at straws, he knew it, but he was desperate. "I have the right to be seen as a separate entity from those flea brains," he went on, thumping himself on the chest. Go for it, Carter. He was really on a roll now. "How dare you prejudge and condemn me. How dare you say I've failed before I've even had the chance to try, to prove to you that I'm not like the others." Brother. Maybe he was overdoing it a bit. "Are all geniuses so narrow-minded, or did you corner the market on that?"

Austin blinked, opened her mouth, then snapped it closed. She opened her mouth and tried again. "Narrow-minded? Me? I've prejudged and condemned you? Me? I did?"

"Yes," he said, attempting to sound extremely peeved as a knot tightened in his stomach.

"I think I'm rather confused. I know what I'm saying is right, because I've been through it, seen it happen. But you're making me sound awful, like a not-very-nice person. I don't know quite what to do."

Love me! Sam wanted to shout. Instead, he said, "It's very simple. You give us a chance to see what we really have together." *Please!* "You live in the here and now instead of making me pay a price for things I didn't do." *Please, Austin?* "If I fail, I'll have only myself to blame. I won't be defeated by ghosts. It's not fair." *I love you, Austin Tyler.* "Well?" he said, turning to look at her.

"I don't know what to say."

"Yes will do nicely. You say, yes, you'll give us a chance. We'll spend time together, talk, share." He'd hold her, kiss her, pretend he never had to let her go. Pretend, hell! He didn't intend to let her go. He was going to marry this woman. "We'll take it slow and easy." Really? he asked himself. He ached to make love to her. He leaned forward and brushed his lips over hers. "Say it, Austin," he murmured. He slid his tongue along her bottom lip and felt her shiver from the feathery foray. "Say it. Say, 'Yes, Sam.' "

"Yes, Sam," she said. "Kiss me again, Sam."

"My pleasure, ma'am. *Our* pleasure."

He placed his large hands on her waist and lifted her onto his lap, claiming her mouth in the next instant. Austin wound her arms around his neck and met his tongue with her own. His hand slipped beneath the edge of her T-shirt, then up over her creamy skin to find one breast. He nestled it in the palm of his hand, his thumb stroking the nipple to a taut button beneath the wispy material of her bra. Blood pounded in his veins, and he ached with the sweet torture of wanting her.

Shimmers of heat swept through Austin, igniting a liquid fire of desire deep within her. She felt a tremor rip through him as his passion grew, and felt the evidence of his need of her pressing against her. Sam. How safe, how protected, how purely feminine she was in his arms.

"I want you, Austin," he said close to her lips.

"Yes, Sam," she mumbled, then her eyes flew wide open. "No, Sam. Good grief, we're in the backyard under an apple tree in broad daylight."

"Oh," he said, glancing around. "You're right. That's where we are." He cleared his throat roughly as he removed his hand from beneath her shirt. "I think perhaps you should go back into the house, poke your cute tush in the air, and paint the baseboards."

"Aren't you coming in?"

"Give me a few minutes. Since this nose on my face is the only one I own, I'd better cool off before Houston or Dallas sees me. Get the picture?"

"I can feel the picture," she said, smiling at him. But then she frowned. "I know you think that we can work around the fact—"

"Hey," he interrupted, "you made a deal. What do I have to do, get you to sign a contract? Where's the part of you that knows how to smile? Seals a deal on your word like my grandfather? We're going out to dinner tonight, Austin. I'll pick you up at eight o'clock. I'd like it very much if you'd wear your hair free, loose, but I'm not telling you what to do." He paused. "Austin, wear your hair free and tumbling down your back."

She laughed. "Okay. It's nice to know you wouldn't try to tell me what to do."

"I wouldn't dream of it," he said, grinning at her. "Now, go, before the dynamic duo comes looking for us, and decides to rearrange my face." He gave her a quick peck on the cheek, then lifted her off of his lap. "Go."

Austin straightened her T-shirt, smiled at Sam, then started toward the house. Sam leaned his head back, closed his eyes, and drew a deep breath, letting it out slowly.

He was exhausted, he realized. Drained. He felt as though he'd just concluded a touch-and-go contract negotiation tougher than any he'd taken on before. He'd been fighting for time. Fighting for Austin. Fighting for his life. And he'd won. For now.

He was on thin ice, and he knew it. He couldn't afford to make mistakes, but wasn't sure how to prevent them because he had no idea as to what he was doing, how to act, what to say to convince Austin that her being a genius wasn't going to destroy what they had.

Control, Sam thought. That's what he needed. He had to reclaim command of himself, set his goals, his purpose, and carry on. That goal was Austin. Austin falling in love with him. Austin agreeing to marry him. Austin committing herself to a lifetime with him and the children they would have. He needed it to accomplish what he intended. Austin Tyler would be his.

"I hope," he said wearily.

Austin walked slowly back to the house, wondering if her eyes, lips, her entire face advertised the fact that she'd been very thoroughly kissed. The best thing to do, she decided, was hurry inside and poke her nose close to the baseboards with her trusty paintbrush in hand. Good plan.

Houston stepped out of the back door.

So much for that, she thought dismally. "Hi," she said, smiling brightly.

Houston crossed his arms over his chest and stared at her, no readable expression on his face. "You look quite chipper."

"Yes. Well, it was nice chatting with you, Houston, but I really must get back to the baseboards. Those little devils won't paint themselves, you know. See ya."

"Nice try, kid," he said, raising his hand to halt her flight past him, "but it didn't work. You ran out of here crying, you've come back smiling. Am I to assume that wonderful things happened with Sam behind that tree?"

Austin sighed. "No. Yes. Well, no. I don't know," she said, throwing up her hands. "It's all so confusing."

"Tell me about it."

"Houston, I should never see Sam Carter again, because it can't possibly work out between us, because I have experience in these matters, and I know what I'm talking about. Sam doesn't believe it, and said I'd prejudged and condemned him and was narrow-minded, which wasn't a very nice thing to say, but he had a point. I guess. Sort of. Anyway, I agreed to give us a chance, which is really stupid, because I'll mess up my memories on top of everything else, but I just couldn't say good-bye to him yet, so we're going out to dinner."

"Austin, as amazing as it is, I understand every word of that. I think you made a very wise decision. I hope you enjoy your dinner."

"Oh."

"Now, go tend to your paintbrush. It's stiff as a board, and I've told you not to leave brushes covered in paint like that."

"Oh."

"Austin!"

"Oh!" She ran into the house. Houston chuckled softly and shook his head.

Sam pushed himself to his feet and started back toward the house, squaring his shoulders as he saw Houston standing by the back door.

What mood was the mountain in now? Sam wondered. Leave it to him to fall in love with a woman who came with matching bodyguards. Huge bodyguards. Bodyguards who had a penchant for breaking noses. Well, that was just too damn bad, because he, Samuel Carter, had no intention of backing off. His program was set, he was once more in control, his purpose was clear. He was going to woo and win Austin Tyler. Forget that. He didn't know how to woo. But woo or not, Austin was going to be his!

Sam narrowed his eyes as he approached Houston, deciding that made him look a tad tougher and might even produce an image of "Don't mess with me, I'm mean."

Then Sam's mouth dropped open in surprise.

A wide smile broke across Houston's face, he gave Sam a thumbs-up sign, then turned and strolled into the house.

Samuel Carter just stood there, looking like a close relative of a goldfish.

Six

At midnight that night Austin wiggled around in bed trying, yet again, for a comfortable position. She flopped over onto her stomach, lasted five seconds, then flipped onto her back. She sighed. Frowned. Then sighed again.

Her evening out with Sam, she decided, had been . . . That was what was making it impossible for her to sleep! She didn't know *what* it had been. Strange? Well, no, not exactly. Dining at an exclusive restaurant, eating delicious food by candlelight wasn't strange. Being told she was a vision of loveliness in her teal blue chiffon dress wasn't strange. A little corny, but not strange. Being in the company of a devastatingly handsome man in a perfectly tailored charcoal-gray suit and a shirt that matched his blue eyes to perfection was super, not strange.

Cancel strange. The evening had been . . . Darn it, why couldn't she get a handle on this? She was a genius, for Pete's sake, was supposed to know how to analyze things, figure them out to the most minute detail.

"That's it!" she said, popping straight up. The evening had been perfectly normal! Austin Tyler had gone out to dinner with Samuel Carter. Sam had not made one reference to the fact that she was a genius, hadn't brought up the subject of the scene under the apple tree, nor pushed her for more details on what it was like to be so awesomely smart.

They had, she now realized, talked, laughed, enjoyed each other's company. Sam had told her about the hilarious pranks he'd pulled on his sister, Marilyn, when the two were growing up. She'd offered stories of Houston and Dallas changing places in classrooms, on dates, and how they'd convinced a crabby newcomer to their block that he was seeing things, when one twin would appear at his front door, the other at the back door seconds later.

They'd discussed movies they'd seen, books they'd read, discovered they both liked mystery novels, then moved on to the subjects of music, their favorite season of the year, what sports they enjoyed.

The hours had flown by. Austin had been a bundle of nerves as she'd waited for Sam to pick her up. She'd lectured herself sternly on the fact that there were to be no dissertations such as the ones she'd delivered previously on refrigerators and bordellos. She would think before she spoke, weigh and measure what she said before she opened her mouth.

But the hours with Sam, she now realized, hadn't gone that way at all. She'd relaxed, relaxed even more, and before she knew it, was having a wonderful time. A normal time. A woman-with-a-man time. Austin with Sam.

At her door Sam had gathered her into his arms, kissed her until she couldn't breathe, then seen her safely inside. Before she could draw enough air into her lungs to speak, he'd said he'd see her the next day, then left her staring blankly at the closed door.

Austin's frown was replaced by a smile. Sam, she mused dreamily. Scrumptious Sam. The evening he had just given her was a precious gift. Only hours after learning of her problem, he'd made certain that their time together was special, but normal. Thoughtful, dear, warm, wonderful Sam.

The frown returned. Now what? she wondered. Glorious stolen hours did not a future make. Playing ostrich would not erase the fact that she was not, would never be, like other people. The bottom line remained the same; she simply did not fit in anywhere on a daily basis, interacting with others. She blew it, time after time.

Now what? She didn't know. What the tomorrows held, she didn't know. What Sam was thinking at that very moment, she didn't know. For a genius, she certainly didn't know much.

Her fingertips came to rest on her lips, to hold

captive the memory of that bone-melting kiss at her door. If she'd been capable of speaking, she'd have said, 'Kiss me again, Sam' and again, and again. Oh, the desire that hummed within her when he held her, touched, kissed her. She could still feel his strong, gentle hand on her breast from their time under the apple tree. Ecstasy.

But she wanted more. Oh, shame on her, but she did. She wanted to be one with Sam, mesh with him, not know where her body left off and his began. She wanted to celebrate a glorious union with him, give all that she was, receive all he would bring to her. She wanted, she needed, to engage in the most intimate act between man and woman, with Sam.

Because she loved him.

There it was.

She'd gone and done it.

She'd fallen in love with Samuel Carter of Carter, Carter, and Carter.

And it was, without a doubt, the dumbest thing she'd ever done.

She'd just custom-ordered herself a broken heart.

Oh, it might work for a while, she thought, she and Sam, together. Tonight had proven that for snatches of time they could be like any other people. But in the long run, in the forever run, it was hopeless. She'd open her mouth, embarrass Sam to death in front of his friends or family with one of her spiels from her data-bank brain, and that would be that.

Her mind was her worst enemy.

But at the moment her heart wasn't exactly her best friend.

Austin waited for the tears to start, decided she must have used up her quota for the day, sighed a soft sigh, and fell asleep.

Samuel Carter was feeling extremely pleased with himself. Even rather smug, he decided. The evening with Austin had gone exactly as he'd planned, come off without a hitch, and in short had been fantastic.

He poured himself a drink, toasted his brilliance, then wandered around his living room, sipping the liquor.

Brilliant, he repeated mentally. Austin had been, as he'd anticipated, nervous when he'd picked her up. Well, he'd been a bit nervous himself, but he'd simply executed his finest control and appeared calm and relaxed. The entire evening had been like a perfectly choreographed dance. Each subject he brought up for discussion was safe, uncomplicated, the stuff that any couple would chat about over a leisurely dinner. Austin had slowly relaxed, started to enjoy herself.

Then at last, *at last*, her eyes had twinkled.

Oh, he'd done a helluva fine job tonight, he told himself, toasting himself again. Samuel Carter in control was awesome to behold.

Austin, he mused. Lord, she'd been beautiful in that dress with her hair shimmering down her back. When he'd kissed her good night at her door, he hadn't wanted to leave, to let her out of his embrace, to return to the big old house alone.

She was a part of him now, an extension of himself, half of his whole. Lord, how he loved her.

And she cared deeply for him, he knew she did. He could see it in her eyes, feel it in the way she responded more each time he kissed her.

But now what? he questioned. Yes, fine, they'd had a terrific evening, but what about tomorrow and all the tomorrows after that? Hell, he wanted to marry Austin Tyler, spend the rest of his life with her. He couldn't program every day of their lives.

"Well, hell," Sam said, slouching onto the sofa. So much for his euphoric mood. He hadn't solved anything tonight, he'd simply postponed attempting to make Austin realize that she must accept herself as she was, just as he did.

And he did accept her as she was, he truly did. Yes, her initial announcement of her intelligence had been a shock, but he didn't feel threatened by it, didn't see it robbing him of any of his masculinity. He had, in fact, found the nutsy information about the bordello totally fascinating.

But how, he wondered, did he undo the damage done to her at that institute? How did he convince her that he loved her just as she was? How did he make her see that while the evening they'd just spent together was lovely, they couldn't go through life playing games, pretending. How did he do all that?

Tomorrow. Tomorrow he'd tell her he loved her. He'd go for the whole shebang, ask her to marry him, talk about babies. Lord, he amazed himself sometimes with the fine-tuned workings of his mind. A man in control was capable of great things.

With a decisive nod and his good mood restored, Sam got to his feet, closed up the house for the night, and went to bed.

The next morning, dressed in jeans and a light-weight sweater, her hair in a single braid, Austin entered the kitchen of her parents' house just as her mother was preparing to leave for church.

"I thought you preferred the evening service," Austin said.

"I have a rush order of prayers to deliver. Once I do that, I won't have to worry about it."

"It? What 'it'? Where's Dad?"

"Dad?" her mother said, raising her eyebrows.

"My father? Your husband?"

"*That* Dad."

"How many do I have?"

"Just one, and he's a darling," Mrs. Tyler said. "I must dash."

"Mom, where is Dad?"

"He's with Houston."

"Progress," Austin said, nodding. "And where is Houston?"

"With your father, silly girl. I swear, Austin, sometimes I don't think you listen to a word I say. 'Bye, dear," she said, kissing the air near Austin's cheek. She nearly ran out the back door.

"John Wayne wouldn't approve of your giving evasive answers, Mother," Austin called after her.

She went to the phone, called Houston, and got

the answering machine. She then phoned Dallas, there was no answer, and she surmised that he was with Joyce.

"Well, darn," she said. She went outside and started toward her apartment.

"Hello," Sam yelled from the top of her stairs.

Oh, hello, Sam. Hello, hello, hello, she thought, knowing she was smiling. "Hello. This is a nice surprise."

"Are you coming up, or should I come down?"

"Want to sit on the bench swing under that tree?"

"You're on," he said, then came down the stairs two at a time. He closed the distance between them and smiled at her. "Who will see us if I kiss you?"

"No one is home."

"You have a very considerate family," he said, cradling her face in his hands.

"Actually, I think two of them are among the missing."

"What?"

"Never mind. I'm just nosy."

"What you are," he said, lowering his head toward hers, "is beautiful." And he loved her.

She was being kissed, Austin thought suddenly, by the man she loved. She was in love with Sam Carter, and he was kissing her, and it was wonderful. This was a special kiss, a memory kiss to be cherished forever. The kiss was also . . . over.

She opened her eyes and looked up at Sam questioningly.

"The swing," he said. "Let's go to the swing. I want to talk to you."

Talking was nice, Austin mused, but she sure could have gone for a few more of those kisses.

They settled onto the swing, leaned back against the wooden slats, and Sam set the swing gently in motion.

Oh, great, he thought, he was nervous. He wanted to be romantic when he told Austin that he loved her, when he asked her to marry him. The setting was perfect, the swing was a nice touch. Now, if he could just get his tongue to work, he'd be all set. Control, Carter. Control. He'd rehearsed his speech while he'd shaved that morning, telling Austin that she was the only woman he'd ever loved, that he was requesting the honor of her hand in marriage, that he would devote his life to making her happy. It was a first-class speech. So, say it!

"Austin?"

"Yes?"

"Austin?"

"Yes, Sam?"

"I . . . um . . . would you like me to push the swing a little faster?" Hell.

"No, it's fine. I throw up if it gets too rocky."

"Oh. Well, I'll try to remember that. Austin?"

"Sam, is something wrong, or have you developed a sudden attachment to the sound of my name?"

"I adore your name."

"Thank you."

"Austin?"

"Sam, for heaven's sake, what is it?"

"Dammit," he shouted, gripping her shoulders. "I love you!" Austin's mouth dropped open. "I love you, I want to marry you, I want to have a baby. No, I want *you* to have the baby. What I mean is, *we'll* have a baby. Yes, dammit, I love you and . . ." His voice trailed off, and his shoulders slumped. "I think I just blew the whole thing."

Austin blinked once very slowly, closed her mouth, then opened it again. "You love me?" she whispered.

"Oh, yes, Austin, I do," he said, his voice husky. "I swear I do. And I want you to marry me, be my wife, stay by my side for the rest of our lives. I want to have children with you, watch them grow up. I want to make love to you at night, and when we wake in the morning. Say yes. Please, Austin, say you'll marry me."

She swallowed and fought against tears that were threatening. "No," she said softly.

"What?"

"No, Sam, I can't marry you. The time I've spent with you has been wonderful, every minute, every second. I'll cherish those memories as though they were precious gems." A tiny sob caught in her throat, but she rushed on. "And I love you, and you're scrumptious, and you make me feel so beautiful, but, no, I can't marry you."

"Whoa!" he said, raising a hand. "Halt. Back up here. You love me?"

"I didn't say that."

"Yes, you did," he said, waggling a finger at her. "Yes, ma'am, you certainly did."

"I did?" she asked, her eyes widening.

"Yep," he said, appearing extremely smug. "It was right smack-dab between the memories being precious gems and the fact that I'm scrumptious. You're dealing with a contract lawyer here," he went on, tapping his temple with his fingertip. "I'm very alert when it comes to details. You definitely said that you love me."

"Oh," she said, in a small voice. "Oh. Well. Oh."

"You're so articulate sometimes," he said, then gave her a quick kiss on the end of her nose. "Ah, Austin," he said softly. "I love you, you love me. There's nothing to keep us from having a wonderful life together."

"Yes, there is! Sam, you're not thinking clearly. I'm not like the other women you've known."

"I know. You have the most beautiful hair I've ever seen, eyes that actually twinkle, and when I kiss you, it's like rockets going off on the Fourth of July."

"That's not what I mean and you know it. My eyes twinkle? No, forget that. Sam, I have a problem, remember? I don't fit in. I wouldn't know how to act or what to say in your circle of friends."

"Then"—he brushed his lips over hers—"we'll stay home." He slid his tongue over her bottom lip. "Together. Just the two of us."

" 'Kay," she said dreamily. In the next instant she stiffened and pushed against his chest. "Stop that, Sam. I can't think when you do that."

"Good," he said, reaching for her again. "Don't think beyond saying that you'll marry me."

She smacked his hands and scooted farther along the swing. "No. No, I can't marry you. And please don't say that our lovely evening out last night proves anything. Yes, it was special and I had a wonderful time, but you very carefully picked the subjects we talked about. You made sure I couldn't go off on a tangent about air conditioners or bordellos, and upset myself."

Damn, Sam thought, she'd figured out what he'd done. Well, what did one expect when one was dealing with a genius?

"Sam," she said in exasperation, throwing up her hands, "don't you see? This just isn't going to work. Your world is beyond me. Think of how horrified your friends would be if I started lecturing about some esoteric subject. We couldn't live like that, wondering when I was going to embarrass you to death."

"Austin, you would never embarrass me. I find all that information you have tucked away in that marvelous brain of yours fascinating, enchanting. A bubblehead might embarrass me. You? Never."

"It wouldn't work," she said, shaking her head.

"Well, wonderful," he said, slouching back and crossing his arms over his chest, a deep frown on his face. "You're just dusting us off, throwing away everything we could have together because *you've* decided it won't work. We love each other, which means we are now officially in a relationship, which means we have equal voices in said relationship, which means we compromise, give and take, which means—"

"You're blithering."

"Well, dammit, what do you expect? You're driving me nuts! I'm in love for the first time in my life. And guess what? The lady loves *me*. But is everything hunky-dory peachy-keen? Hell, no. I'm being shown the door before I hardly got inside. Why? Because you're too scared to come out from behind walls you've built around yourself. And I can't break down those walls, Austin. You're going to have to meet me halfway, trust me, believe in yourself." He gripped her upper arms. "You wouldn't be alone," he said, his voice gentling. "I'd be there; I'd be with you every step of the way. Look, don't give me an answer about marrying me. We'll put that on hold. Just agree to go places with me, meet my family and friends, try new things. We'll take it slow and easy. Okay?"

"I have to think."

He dropped his hands. "Go ahead. Think your little heart out. Just make sure you come up with the right answer."

Austin glared at him, then stared up at the sky. Goodness, goodness, goodness, she thought, Sam loved her. Sam wanted to marry her. *Her*. But, oh, dear heaven, it wouldn't work. He had no idea what she'd been through in the past few years; trying so hard to fit in, and failing miserably time after time. He just didn't understand.

But if she stood firm in what she knew to be true, Sam would get up from that swing and walk out of her life forever. She couldn't bear that.

What if she agreed to his plan to take her into his social circle? He'd discover soon enough that it was a mistake. But if she agreed to do it, she was going to muster her courage and be herself.

"Okay," she said at last, "I'll try it. But I have to warn you, Sam. If I'm going to be brave enough to meet the people you know, I'm going to do it as Austin Tyler, the genius. I'm just going to be myself, exactly as I am."

"Perfect," he said, smiling at her.

Ha! she thought.

"We have a bargain, a deal," Sam said. "We need to seal it officially."

"Good grief, are you going to draw up a contract for me to sign?"

"Nooo," he said slowly, "this is going to be done like those who know how to smile. We're going to seal our bargain with a kiss."

"How nice," Austin said, smiling brightly. "Your grandfather and my mother would be proud of us."

He gathered her into his arms. "I love you, Austin," he said, then his mouth melted over hers.

He drew back after savoring their intimacy. "Austin," he said, "it's incredible what a kiss shared with you does to me."

" 'Kiss' is a modern English word originating from the Middle English 'kissen.' In Old English it was 'cyssan.' It is also akin to Old High German 'kussen,' meaning 'to kiss.' "

Sam threw his head back and roared with laughter as he continued to hold Austin tightly in his arms.

"You're sensational," he said, smiling at her. "I love you, Austin Tyler, I truly do."

"Oh, Sam, I love you, too, but . . ." She sighed.

"Shh," he said, then claimed her mouth once more.

The kiss was long and powerful, and Austin was trembling in Sam's arms when he finally released her. His breathing was rough, and neither spoke for several minutes.

"Want to go shopping?" he said finally.

"For what?"

"Furniture. I looked at the stuff I have in my apartment and decided I was tired of it. I'll sublease the place furnished. Then I'll pitch out the worst of what's in the house and start from there. I'm keeping the bed. After all, that's where I met you."

"Sam, don't ever say that where anyone could hear. It sounds terrible."

He chuckled. "It does? Wait until I tell everyone about the red walls and the mirrors."

"No comment."

They drove into Chicago and went to countless stores, comparing styles, fabrics, colors, and costs. Austin kept notes on a pad of paper and each room of Sam's house was assigned a page. She remembered the exact shade of paint that was to be used where, and informed Sam that they must accomplish an overall affect of coordination while still reflecting his personality. A salesman rolled his eyes when Austin insisted an examining the joints of each chair to a dining room set, the man claiming they were all of the finest quality.

Austin shot him a withering look, and proceeded with her exploration. Sam just smiled.

When Sam finally moaned that he was exhausted, Austin hauled him into a café to review her findings. Final selections were made of a sofa, chairs, end tables, lamps, and the dining room set that had passed her inspection. Since the items came from four different stores, Austin went to the ladies lounge and used the phone there to arrange the purchases. She even managed to co-ordinate all the delivery schedules for a four-hour period on the same day so as not to continually disrupt the crew of Tyler Construction.

And as Samuel heard all this, he just kept on smiling.

They picked up Chinese food for dinner and headed back to Sam's.

She was something, he thought as he drove. Austin was really something. She was a master of efficiency and detail, capable of smoothly organizing the most complicated project. He'd watched her closely through the day, had seen the twinkle in her eyes, the genuine smile on her lips. She'd thoroughly enjoyed herself. Yet he knew that if he asked her, she would see no connection between what she had done and her level of intelligence.

He realized more and more that Austin saw her genius only as a liability. He had to make her realize that what she had done that day, and had had fun doing, was a direct result of her intelligence. She must come to learn that there were rewards attached to her gift. She wasn't a freak, she was a marvel, and she could pick and choose where she wished to apply her unique talents.

In the kitchen at Sam's they made short work of the Chinese food, Sam declaring that shopping was extremely hard work and they deserved second helpings of everything the multitude of little white boxes offered.

After dinner they went into the living room and had a loud debate on where the new furniture should be placed. Sam had no idea what should go where, but he was enjoying himself so much, he argued with everything that Austin said. At one point she punched him playfully on the shoulder, and he whipped his arm around her waist and pulled her up against him.

And everything changed.

The amusement in their eyes faded and was replaced by the smoky hues of desire. Hearts beat in wild rhythms. Neither spoke, moved, seemed to breathe.

"I think . . ." Samuel started, his voice raspy, "that I'd better take you home now. I don't want to, Austin, but it would be the best thing to do. I want you, pure and simple. After spending such a great day with you, having you near me, I want to end these hours by making love to you. And so I'm going to take you home."

"No," she said. What? What was she saying? She knew what would happen if she stayed.

"What?"

"No, Sam. I don't want to go home now," she said, her voice hushed. Yes, this felt right and good. This was where she wished to be that night.

There. With Sam. "I want to stay. I want to make love with you, Sam."

He drew a deep shuddering breath. "Are you sure? Austin, please, be certain that you're ready to take this step with me."

"I'm very sure, Sam. I promise you that."

"Ah, Austin." He groaned, then brought his mouth down hard onto hers. When he lifted his head he gazed directly into her eyes. "I love you, Austin Tyler."

"And I love you, Sam Carter. Tonight is ours."

He circled her shoulders with his arm and led her up the stairs.

More then tonight would be theirs, Sam vowed. The future was theirs, the rest of their lives. Austin was giving herself to him that night, and he was never, ever, going to let her go.

Seven

In the bedroom Sam switched on the small lamp on the nightstand, and in the next instant both he and Austin glanced up at the hole in the ceiling, then at each other with matching smiles.

"It'll make a great story to tell our grandchildren," Sam said. Austin's smile faded. "Hey, come here." He drew her close to his chest.

An involuntary sigh of pleasure whispered from Austin's lips as she nestled close to him. She tilted her head back as Sam lowered his, and their lips met. Her thoughts skidded to an abrupt halt, and she felt, only felt. Sam.

Sam felt the hot rush of desire in his body, causing his blood to pound in his veins, and his manhood to stir. A wave of virile impatience swept through him—raging want and need, the wild urge to become one with the woman in his embrace. The only woman he had ever loved.

The kiss deepened, and Samuel slid his hands over the slope of Austin's buttocks, fitting her to him as he spread his legs slightly to bring her closer yet. A groan rumbled up from his chest.

He lifted his head and trailed a ribbon of kisses down Austin's throat as his hands moved to the waistband of her sweater. He inched it upward and felt her move back with no hesitation to give him room to draw it up and away. He let it drop to the floor, then removed her bra. His heart thundered as he gazed at her small, firm breasts.

"Oh, Austin," he said, filling his palms with her breasts. He lowered his head. "You're exquisite." He drew one nipple into his mouth, his tongue flicking the bud to a taut button. He moved to the other breast—sucking, tasting, drinking of her sweetness.

Austin gripped Sam's shoulders for support as her legs began to tremble. She closed her eyes to savor and memorize each glorious sensation rocketing through her. Oh, she felt so alive and vital, so aware of every inch of her own body and of Sam's, of the marvelous differences between man and woman, and the sensual promise that difference held.

Samuel stepped behind her and took the rubber band from the end of the thick braid. He slowly, reverently, drew his fingers through the twisted hair, freeing it, sifting it, burying his face in its fragrance. He moved in front of her again, lifting the heavy tresses forward to fall over her breasts.

"Oh, Austin, you are so beautiful," he said, awe evident in his voice.

"I'm glad you think so, Sam," she said, her voice hushed. "You're the only one that matters."

With perfect balance she removed first one shoe, then the other. She unzipped her jeans and slid them down her slender legs, taking her bikini panties as she went. She stepped clear of the pool of clothes, straightened, and faced Sam.

With visibly shaking hands, Samuel unbuttoned his shirt, pulled it free of his pants, then shrugged out of it. He hesitated a moment at his belt buckle, then proceeded as Austin watched closely every move he made. Within moments he was naked and her gaze traveled slowly over him, his skin seeming to burn along the trail made by her eyes. His manhood was a bold announcement of his need of her, his aching want to be one with her. He felt strangely vulnerable, and a trickle of sweat ran down his back.

"You are magnificent," Austin said, looking directly into his blue eyes. "You are the most beautiful man I have ever seen."

Sam released a rush of pent-up breath, only then realizing he'd been holding it. Never in his life, he realized, had he been so aware of his own body, of how rough and rugged it was compared to Austin's soft curves. Of how tall and strong he was, and how frightening he could appear as he stood before her fully aroused. Her acceptance of him, of all that he was, meant more to him than he'd ever imagined possible.

He swept back the blankets on the bed, lifted Austin onto the cool sheets, and stretched out next to her. He splayed his hand on her flat stomach, and his mouth drifted down over hers.

"Oh, Sam," Austin murmured, sure she had never even dreamed that she could feel so heavenly.

"I'll try not to rush you," he said, forcing himself to keep tight control over himself. "I *won't* rush you. This will be perfect for you, Austin. This is for you."

"It's for us, it's ours, together, Sam."

His answer was to claim her mouth once more as his hand skimmed lower, over one thigh to her knee. To the other knee, up across that thigh. He flattened his palm on the nest of auburn curls at the junction of her legs, his fingers inching into the moist secrets of her womanhood. His body bowed after he lifted his lips from hers, and his mouth sought her breast. He drew the nipple deep into his mouth. His sucking matched the tantalizing rhythm of his fingers that were strong yet so gentle.

Austin's breath quickened as the blood sang in her veins. She was awash with desire, the pulsing heat deep inside her keeping tempo with the movement of Sam's fingers and the pulling of his mouth on her breast. Sensations flooded her; waves of passion swept through her like liquid fire, flames, heat, building within her.

"Sam," she gasped.

He shifted to her other breast to pay homage to the sweet flesh. His muscles trembled from forced restraint, his body glistened with perspiration. Every inch of his being screamed for release, anticipated the moment when he would sheath himself in Austin's honeyed warmth. But still he held back. It had to be perfect. She had to be ready for him. She was so small, and he was a big man. He couldn't, *wouldn't*, hurt her.

"Sam, please," Austin said, a sob in her voice.

Not yet! he told himself. He'd always had control of his actions, even at times like this. But, dear heaven, never before had he been consumed with such passion, such a driving, aching need. Because never before had he made love to the woman he loved. To Austin.

Control.

"Sam, oh, Sam, please."

"Soon. Soon. I've got to be sure you're ready for me, Austin. It has to be perfect for you, don't you understand?"

Austin struggled against the hazy passion clouding her mind and listened, really listened, to Sam. Something was wrong. There was a frantic edge to his voice, a sound of near desperation. A shudder ripped through him as he continued his maddening, sweet torture of her body. His muscles quivered from the restraint he was forcing upon himself.

And Austin's heart nearly burst with love.

Never in her life had she felt so loved, so cherished, so special. He was giving, and giving, and giving, she knew, so that she would be the one to take, receive. He was exerting that control he was so proud of.

No, Austin thought, desire fierce within her. They were together and sharing; they were equals. She didn't wish just to receive, she wanted to give as well. What Sam was doing was dear, and sweet, and wonderful. And wrong.

Austin slipped her hand between their moist bodies and gently cradled Sam's throbbing manhood. He jerked his head up as he drew a sharp, painful breath.

"Austin, don't," he said hoarsely. "I'm hanging on by a thread."

"Come to me, Sam," she said in a seductive whisper. "Love me, become one with me. I want you, Sam. Now."

He moaned, the sound seeming to come from the very depths of his soul. He moved over her and into her. She arched her back to meet him, to draw him deeper within her heat as she wrapped her arms around his back.

And Samuel Carter lost control.

"Oh, Austin!"

He plunged within her. Deeper he went. Harder. Taking her above all that was reality and carrying her to a place of swirling colors and heightened sensations. Ecstasy. Higher. She was filled with him, and fulfilled by him as she flew closer and closer to the sun. Then . . .

"Sam!"

"Yes," he gasped. "Oh, yes."

He thrust once more deep within her, then joined

her in the place of shattering pleasure, the essence of all that he was pulsing into the sweet haven of her body. He collapsed against her, spent, breathing heavily, his heart matching the thundering of hers. With his last ounce of strength Sam rolled to his side, taking Austin with him, their bodies still meshed as one entity. He rested his lips on her moist forehead and brushed her hair away from her face.

Neither spoke as they drifted back to where they started, each memorizing the beauty of where they had been. Together.

"I love you," Sam finally said. "You were wonderful."

"*We* were wonderful," she said, then kissed the damp curly hair on his chest.

"Did I hurt you?"

"No."

"You sort of took matters into your own hands," he said, chuckling softly. "Literally."

"I knew what you were doing, Sam. It was so dear of you, so generous. But I wanted to give to you too. I wanted us to be together, really together. Are you angry?"

"Lord, no. You just taught me, my little genius, that there are times when my control gets in the way. I thought I was doing the right thing, but you were the wiser, and I love you for it. Oh, Austin, I will never forget this night. And it's only one of a million to come."

Oh, Sam, don't, Austin thought. She didn't want him to speak of the future, of the tomorrows. She just wanted to cherish this moment, savor it, tuck it away among her precious gems of memories.

Sam reached for the sheet and covered their cooling bodies. They gave way to the somnolence that claimed them, and slept.

The soft rosy glow of dawn inched beneath the drapes on the window, and crept like insistent fingers over Sam's face. He opened his eyes and was immediately aware of the warm bundle curled up next to him.

Austin.

He gazed at her, admitting to himself that the smile on his face undoubtedly made him look like a lovesick teenager, but not caring. Austin. Lord, how he loved her. And how incredibly beautiful their lovemaking had been. Austin had given herself to him so totally, trustingly, freely.

He knew, as he pieced together the picture of her life, that she was not very experienced. Her response to him had been honest, real, the result of womanly instincts awakened by his touch. And with that womanly wisdom had come the knowledge that what they were to share should be just that . . . shared. Because of her forcing him to lose control, their union had been like none he had ever known before.

Sam feasted his eyes on the silken, tumbled disarray of Austin's hair, on her delicate features, her slightly parted lips. The sheet just barely covered her breasts, and heat shimmered through him as he trailed his gaze over her lissome form outlined beneath the thin material. He felt the stirring of his manhood, the renewed ache of desire, and wondered what Austin would do if he woke her at such an early hour.

Before he could decide whether to risk waking her, he jerked in surprise as he felt nimble fingers walking up his stomach to his chest, and heard a bubble of laughter burst in the air.

"You're awake," he said.

Austin opened her eyes and smiled at him. "I always wake up when someone is leering at me."

"I wasn't leering," he said indignantly. "I was simply appreciating the view."

"Oh." She walked her fingers back down the path she'd taken, then lower, and lower.

"Austin!"

"Yes?" she asked, all playful innocence.

"You have three hours to stop doing that."

She laughed. "Oh, okay. You just doze, and I'll explore. Here . . . and here . . . and, oh, my, right here."

Sam groaned.

"Love me, Sam," she whispered. "I want you."

"You can't possibly be ready for me yet. I'll hurt you."

"Trust me. Come to me, Sam."

The hell with control, Sam thought.

He entered her with a powerful thrust that brought a gasp of pleasure from Austin's lips. He captured the passionate sound in his mouth and met her tongue as he drove deep within her. Austin wrapped her legs around his, urging him on, lifting her hips to receive all that he was. They soared. Spasms of ecstasy rippled through them only seconds apart as they called to each other, clung to each other, gave and received from each other. They drifted. Sighed in contentment. Returned.

"Oh . . . my," Austin said rapturously.

"Well said," Sam murmured into her hair. "Lord, I love being inside you like this. I think I'll just stay here."

"Mmm," she said, tightening her hold on his strong back.

They remained like that for several more minutes, Sam supporting his weight on his forearms.

"Duty calls," he said finally with a sigh. "I have an early appointment."

"And I," Austin said, laughing softly, "have to meet Houston and Dallas so that I can come back over here to work on the house. I need to go home first for fresh clothes. Oh, and I need a shower, and I'm hungry."

"Anything else?" he said, lifting his head to smile at her.

"Well . . ." she said slowly, wiggling beneath him.

"Oh, no, you don't," he said, leveling himself off her. "You have a way of starting things that I'm only too happy to finish. At this rate we'll never get out of this bed." He paused. "Now that I think about it, that isn't such a bad idea."

Austin laughed in delight and was rewarded with a hard, searing kiss. As Sam disappeared into the bathroom, she stretched leisurely with a sigh of contentment. Oh, how she loved Sam Carter, she mused. Their lovemaking had been like nothing she had ever experienced before.

Not, she admitted, that she was exactly very experienced, but she knew that their union had been beyond description in its beauty. And for Sam, too, it had been special, she was sure of it. He had stepped over that invisible line he kept himself on, and given all of himself to her. Together they had become one complete whole.

If only they didn't have to go beyond the walls of that house. If only they could stay close, centered on each other, forgetting there was a world outside waiting for them. Despite Sam's conviction that they would have a future, a wonderful lifetime together, she knew better. Her glaring problem, her inability to fit in, was going to catch up to them and shatter all that they had into a million pieces.

"Oh, hell," she said, then tossed back the blankets on the bed. She wouldn't dwell on it now. She was still tingling from head to toe in the aftermath of Sam's exquisite lovemaking, and she intended to savor every moment. She'd face harsh reality later, when she had no choice.

Austin reached for her clothes, deciding to wait until she got home to shower so that she could put on fresh things. She pulled a brush from her purse, managed to untangle her thick hair, then headed downstairs to make coffee.

Much too soon, in Austin's opinion, she was driving toward Houston's. Sam had appeared in the kitchen in a three-piece brown suit with a tan shirt and brown tie. He was, she had informed him, scrumptious. They'd had a quick cup of coffee, then he'd driven her home. Their parting kiss was long and powerful, and Austin had climbed the steps to her apartment on trembling legs. She showered, dressed, and braided her hair. Now, as usual, she was driving to Houston's for the morning meeting.

But she felt different, she realized. Everything around her was sharper, clearer, her senses more alert. She was viewing familiar things as though seeing them for the first time. Her own body was sore where it had never been before, bringing a smile of remembrance to her lips as she thought of Sam's hands and mouth exploring every inch of her. The sky was bluer, the sun brighter, the birds were singing a happier song. Oh, being in love and loved in return was wonderful!

For now.

"Oh, darn," she said, smacking the steering wheel with her hand. Quit thinking, she told herself. She deserved to cherish the memories of the night shared with Sam. And she would.

She pulled to a stop behind Dallas's truck, hurried to the door, knocked, then entered.

"Hi, Dallas," she said.

"Hi, kid. Coffee?"

"Sure."

He handed her a mug, then they sat down at the table.

"Houston isn't here," he said.

Austin's mug stopped halfway to her mouth. "He's not? His truck is here. He's never done this before."

Dallas shrugged. "I figure he had a date with some gal who wasn't into riding in a truck, and they went in her car. Whoever she is, she was more interesting than breakfast. He'll be along."

"I don't know, Dallas," Austin said, frowning. "Mom was acting very strange yesterday when I saw her. She was vague on the subject of where Dad was, would only say he was with Houston."

Dallas smiled. "Mom always acts a little strange. Seen Scrumptious Sam?"

If she blushed, she'd die, Austin thought. Just fall over on her face and die. "Who?" she said, above the rim of her mug.

"You're blushing."

"I am not. Women my age don't blush. That's absurd. Did you hear a car?"

Dallas brushed back the curtain on the window. "Hey, it's Dad and Houston. Houston has a bandage or something on his nose. I wonder what's up?"

"I knew something was going on," Austin said.

The door burst open and a glowering Houston stomped into the room. Teddy Tyler strolled in behind him, a wide grin on his face. Austin and Dallas were up and on their feet.

"Don't speak to me," Houston roared. "Not one damn word. Is there coffee in this place?"

"Yes, but—" Austin started.

"I said don't speak to me," Houston said, pointing a long finger at her.

"Heavens," she said, taking a step backward. She redirected her attention to her father. "Dad, what's going on? Where have you two been? What happened to Houston's nose?"

Houston came out of the kitchen, muttered an earthy expletive, handed his father a cup of coffee, then slouched onto a chair.

"Well, darling girl," Teddy said, chuckling, "Houston and I had some unfinished business to attend to."

"Where?" Austin said.

"At the institute," Teddy said.

"What?" Austin yelled.

"Don't get all in an uproar," her father said, sitting down at the table. "It was long overdue. Those folks needed to be made to understand that they weren't to bother you anymore. My calls and letters weren't doing a bit of good, so . . ." He took a sip of coffee.

"You went without me?" Dallas asked. "Why in the hell did you go without me? Austin is my sister, too, you know."

"You have enough on your plate at the moment, son," Teddy said. "Houston and I took care of it."

"Oh, really?" Austin said, planting her hands on her hips. "And just who took care of Houston's nose? Is it broken? Is that nose broken?"

"Yep," Teddy said, laughing.

"Hell," Houston said.

"You're kidding," Dallas said, grinning.

"I don't believe this," Austin said, rolling her eyes to the heavens.

"Well, you see," Teddy said, "it seems that ever since Houston carried you out of there four years ago, they've had security guards around. Houston scared the begeebers out of those folks back then. Anyway, we skittered past those big lummoxes with no problem, and went looking for that director fella who's been hounding you to come back."

"Oh, goodness," Austin said, sinking into a chair. "Do I want to hear this?"

"No," Houston said.

"Yes," Dallas said. "Go on, Dad."

"Well, we found the little twit, and he was conducting a tour for four or five people, showing off the place. We caught enough of the conversation to know they were megabucks types being asked to donate to the institute. We figured the director would be only too happy to see us in private rather than have us complaining in front of potential check-writers."

"And?" Austin said.

"It didn't quite go that way," Teddy said, stroking his chin. "That twit was so livid when he saw Houston, he clean forgot about the money people and ordered us to clear out of there. I told him, in well-chosen words, what would happen to him and certain parts of his anatomy if he ever contacted you again."

"Oh, Lord," Austin said.

"All right," Dallas said. "Way to go."

"Hell," Houston said again.

"Then, there she was," Teddy said.

"She?" Austin said. "She who?"

"The money lady," Teddy said. "Oh, she was a beauty, pretty as a picture, I'm telling you. She marched up and asked right in that director's face if what we had said was true. She demanded to know if someone had chosen to leave the institute and was being harassed to come back. She was something, all spit and fire. The twit just sputtered and fumbled. Suddenly he reached over to the wall and smacked an alarm button."

"Uh-oh," Dallas said.

"Ohhh," Austin moaned.

"There they came," Teddy went on, "four big bruisers ready to wipe the floor with us."

"Oh, Houston," Austin said sympathetically, "they broke your nose?"

"Hell," Houston said.

Teddy roared with laughter. "Not exactly. See, the rich folks took off running for the hills, except for the pretty little gal. She was furious to think that the director had called in his muscle. I decked one guy, Houston took out two more, then . . ." He dissolved in a fit of laughter.

"Dammit, Dad," Houston said, "knock it off."

"What happened?" Dallas said. "By my count there's one guard left."

"Yep," Teddy said, wiping tears of merriment from his cheeks. "One left, and that little lady decided he was all hers. She made a fist, pulled back her arm, and—"

"Damn it to hell!" Houston said.

"—And," Teddy said, "Houston stepped in front of her to protect her just as she let it fly."

"Oh, Lord," Dallas said, whooping with laughter. "*She* broke his nose?"

"Oh," Austin said. She tried not to smile. She

tried very hard not to smile, but lost the battle. "Oh, my," she said, unable to contain her laughter. "When I think of all the noses that Houston has broken, and his was finally done in by a . . . oh, my."

"I've had it with you people," Houston said. "I'm in pain, you know, but do you care? Hell, no. Just have a good laugh. Enjoy yourselves. Have a ball."

"Oh, Houston, I'm sorry," Austin said. "I love you and Dad for what you did. You probably shouldn't have done it, but I love you anyway. Thank you. I'm really very sorry you were hurt. Was she really beautiful?"

Houston stared into space. "Like a vision. A dream. Like no woman I've ever seen before."

"Uh-oh," Dallas said, smiling into his mug.

"She got us out of jail," Teddy said.

"Out of who?" Austin said, her eyes widening.

"Jail," Teddy said calmly. "Which is where they tossed us, you see. But she showed up with her highfalutin lawyer and got us out. Land's sake, that little gal is something."

"January," Houston said, a wistful tone to his voice.

"Pardon me?" Austin said.

"That's her name. January St. John. Lord, Lord, Lord," he said, shaking his head. Then he moaned loudly, "Oh, my nose. I'm dying."

"What a lovely name," Austin said. "January St. John. Classy."

"She was that," Teddy said, nodding. "First class all the way. She took us to the airport in her chauffeur-driven limousine. She couldn't have been any older than Houston and Dallas, but she sure had a lot of people jumping when she spoke. I've never met anyone like her before. She was rich as can be, but . . . It's hard to explain. She didn't act rich. She wasn't snooty. She had the trappings of money—expensive clothes, the limo, but she acted normal. Yep, she was something."

"Yeah," Houston said, staring off into space again.

"And I say 'Uh-oh,' " Dallas said, grinning at his father. Teddy winked at him.

"Does Mom know about this yet?" Austin said.

"Oh, sure," Teddy said. "I called her from the jail. She said I should invite that nice girl to dinner, even if she did break Houston's nose. Well," he said, getting to his feet, "I'd better head on home."

"Wait a minute," Dallas said softly. "As long as we're all here, there's something I need to tell you. You can explain it to Mom, Dad."

"All right, Dallas," Teddy said. "What is it?"

"I . . . well, I've decided to . . . I realize I'm messing up Houston and Austin but—"

"And I thought I was the only one who blithered," Austin said. "You're going to Tucson with Joyce and Willie because you love them. Right?"

"Yeah. Joyce and I are getting married. But, oh, man, I feel so guilty about Tyler Construction."

"Hey, no way," Houston said, getting to his feet. "Oh, my nose, my head. Listen, brother, I'm happy for you, green with envy, in fact. Austin and I will be fine. You concentrate on Joyce. Just think, you get a son too. Damn, you're a lucky devil."

Dallas got to his feet, and Houston gave him a hug, as did Teddy, then Austin. There was an unusual glistening brightness in the four sets of brown eyes.

"So?" Houston said. "When do you leave?"

"As soon as we finish the job at Sam's," Dallas said. "Joyce has to report to her new job. We'll have to postpone a honeymoon for now. Besides, I'm broke. I'll wait until I can afford to take her someplace great. Houston, about Tyler Construction—"

"Dallas, don't," Houston said. "We gave it our best shot. What you have with Joyce is more important."

"That's right, Dallas," Austin said. "I wasn't that terrific at construction, anyway."

"But what will you do, Austin?" Dallas asked.

"Don't worry about it," she said, then kissed him on the cheek. "Oh, I'm so happy for you."

"Thank you," Dallas said, looking at the toe of his shoe.

"You're blushing. You're blushing," Austin said merrily. "Oh, I love it." Dallas glared at her.

"Well, we'd better get over to Sam's," Houston said. "We're really running late here. I do believe, however, that I'll take two aspirin before we go. I should find every guy whose nose I ever busted and apologize. This bugger really hurts."

"January St. John must pack quite a wallop," Austin said.

"Hell," Houston said, leaving the room.

"She packs a wallop, all right," Teddy said, smiling. "In more ways than one. Well, I'm off to see my sweetheart of a wife. Congratulations again, Dallas. I'm pleased for you, son. Your mother will be thrilled that you're to live out west in John Wayne country. Lord knows we'll miss you, though. Talk to you later."

"Dad," Austin said, "thank you for what you did at the institute."

"I enjoyed every minute of it, darling girl. 'Bye for now."

"Let's hit the road," Houston said, coming back into the room.

"Are you sure you're up to working?" Austin said.

"Yeah. I mean, what's a little pain, excruciating pain, mind-blinding pain, to a rugged man like me?"

"Oh, for cripe's sake," Dallas said, "spare me."

A loud debate started between Houston and Dallas regarding the pain, or lack thereof, involved in having a broken nose. Austin sat between them in the truck and tuned them out, listening instead to the voices in her own mind.

No more Tyler Construction, she thought frantically. She was happy for Dallas, she really was, but . . . Houston could pick and choose any job he wanted. Granted, he was giving up his dream of having his own company, but he was in demand, was sought after by construction crews. He fit in.

What on earth was she going to do? she wondered. Oh, heavens, so much was happening so quickly in her life that her head was spinning. Her days as a part of Tyler Construction were numbered. Her days . . . and nights . . . with her wonderful Sam were numbered, whether he was willing to believe that or not. It would be over, everything. She'd be so alone and lonely.

She wanted to go find Sam right now, she decided. She yearned to be held in his strong arms, feel safe, protected, special, and wanted. But she couldn't do that. All she could do was cherish each precious gem of her memories in the days ahead until it all was over.

And after that, she'd cry.

Eight

It seemed to Austin that the next two weeks passed in a blur of exhausting activity.

The trio of Tyler Construction worked from dawn until dusk on Sam's house to meet Dallas's deadline. Sam would often arrive home to find them still laboring, would change his clothes and grab a paintbrush. But from time to time he'd pull Austin into a shadowed corner and kiss her until her knees trembled.

"You're blushing!" Dallas would yell when Austin reappeared.

Austin would glare.

Dallas and Houston would laugh themselves silly.

Samuel Carter would simply seem extremely pleased with himself.

The story of the trip to the institute was retold, much to Houston's chagrin, for Sam's benefit. In

Dallas's version, however, January St. John had decked a two-hundred-pound guard, *then* managed to break Houston's nose.

Samuel had thoroughly enjoyed the recounting of the tale, then later took Houston aside and thanked him for removing the institute from Austin's life once and for all.

"It had to be done, Sam," Houston said. "I could have lived without this broken nose—do you have any idea how painful a broken nose is?—but, anyway, we did what we had to do. It was a ghost hanging over Austin. It had to be stopped."

"I realize that, and I'm grateful," Sam said. "I guess the rest is up to me."

"Oh?"

"I love her, Houston. I love her, and I want to marry her."

"I'll be damned," he said, a wide grin on his face.

"And Austin loves me. Thing is, she still feels that her being a genius is going to keep us from having a future together. Dammit, she's wrong, and I'm going to prove it to her just as soon as things calm down around here. I realize Dallas's plans have top priority right now, and that's fine. Once he's squared away, Austin is going to keep her part of our deal."

"What deal?"

"She's going to meet my family and friends. She's warned me that she'll do so as herself, as a genius, not holding back on what she might say. She feels that by doing that I'll soon discover that she doesn't fit in. She's wrong."

"Is she?" Houston said quietly. "I've seen it myself, Sam. I've seen people get edgy, seen them look at her like she was a freak."

"I won't give her up," Sam said firmly. "I swear to heaven, I won't give her up."

"Love sure is something to behold," Houston said, shaking his head.

"Your day will come, buddy," Sam said. "It sneaks up on you and lays you flat out. Women are incredible creatures. Speaking of incredible, how much does this January St. John weigh? To have broken your nose, she must look like a fullback."

Houston stared into space, a dopey grin on his face. "She is *beautiful*."

Sam passed his hand back and forth in front of Houston's eyes, and didn't get a flicker.

Sam chuckled, "You're a goner."

"Huh?"

"Nothing," he said, still smiling. "You'll figure it out."

Sam's house was slowly transformed into a creation of beauty, class, and style. The outside was painted off-white with dark brown shutters, the yards kept neat by a crew hired to tend to them once a week.

The new furniture arrived, some of the old removed and some kept to blend in. The ceiling in Sam's bedroom was repaired, and Austin and Sam stood hand in hand and bid the gaping hole a fond farewell.

Teddy Tyler began to show up to help, and

passed instant approval on Austin's Scrumptious Sam.

The work continued.

The days flew by.

The nights, however, as far as Austin was concerned, were a dud.

There was no opportunity for her and Sam to be alone in his wonderful big bed. She was so tired by the end of the day that one of the Tyler men would shovel her into a truck and take her home. On more than one occasion Houston slept on Sam's sofa after working inside the house well past midnight.

Sam had to go to Los Angeles for three days, and Austin missed him so much, in spite of his nightly calls, that her stomach hurt from the constant knot of loneliness.

With each passing day Dallas became more nervous and crabby, and everyone stayed out of his way.

It was a zoo, Austin declared. A ridiculous zoo.

But part of her also knew it was a reprieve from the inevitable. Kisses in the shadows from Sam were better than nothing.

And then the house was completed. It was a masterpiece, a candidate for *House Beautiful,* a place any man would be proud to call home. Every inch, top to bottom, corner to corner, inside and out, was perfect.

Sam opened the finest champagne that money could buy and poured glasses full all around. He toasted the best construction crew on the face of the earth, his gaze riveted on Austin. It was a bittersweet moment, as everyone in the room knew that as of that minute, there was no more Tyler Construction Company.

Dallas's wedding to Joyce was held in judge's chambers with only the Tylers and Sam in attendance, as Joyce had no family. Her son Willie announced three times during the ceremony that he had to go to the bathroom, causing the judge to rattle off the standard phrases like a record set on high speed. Austin thought it was absolutely beautiful, and wept her way through the entire thing.

After a boisterous lunch at an exclusive restaurant, Mr. and Mrs. Dallas Tyler and son changed their clothes, climbed into the cab of a huge U-Haul truck, and started their journey west.

Sam and Austin went to his house, closed the door on the world, and made sweet, slow, sensuous love.

The next day was a repeat performance, and Austin was sure she would burst with sheer joy. Never had she been so happy, so fulfilled, felt so loved, special, or beautiful. It was just the two of them. Austin and Sam. And there was no world beyond their front door.

Then on Monday morning Sam brought her back to reality with a jarring thud.

"I want to have a party," he said. He was dressed for work and sitting opposite her at the kitchen table as they drank coffee. Austin was wearing nothing more than one of his shirts.

"What?" she said, feeling the color drain from her face.

"Saturday night. You won't have to do a thing, I'll handle it. Just be here, be beautiful, be mine."

"A party," she repeated slowly.

"Yes. I have a lovely home now, you know. I want to show it off. And I want everyone to meet the woman I love."

"You do?"

He covered her hand with his on the top of the table. "Austin," he said gently, "it's time, you know that. Things were put on hold because of Dallas, but there's nothing standing in our way now. We have an agreement, you and I, and we're moving forward with it."

"But—"

"I've got to get going," he said, rising to his feet. "Remember, you agreed to not even think about looking for a job for a couple of weeks. You're all worn out from the work you did on this place. Come here, Austin mine, and kiss me good-bye."

Austin moved into Sam's embrace and returned his searing kiss eagerly, wanting more, wanting to drag him back upstairs to bed and forget, just forget, there was a world waiting outside.

"Whew," he said, smiling as he lifted his head. "I will most definitely be home by six, not a second later. I love you, Austin."

"I love you too, Sam," she whispered.

Austin didn't move, even after she heard the door close and the sound of Sam driving away from the house. She felt frozen in place, hardly able to breathe. She wanted time to stop, not go beyond the next beat of her racing heart, not allow the hours and days to pass and force her to face Saturday night.

A party.

On Saturday morning, Sam told Austin to go home.

"Well, that's not very nice," she said, frowning at him.

"I know you. If you stay, you'll work. The caterers will be setting up the buffet, and you'll be right in there helping and organizing. I don't want you worn out before this shindig even starts. I want you to enjoy yourself tonight."

"Fat chance," she muttered.

"What?"

"Nothing."

"Houston will pick you up at seven-thirty," Samuel said.

"Houston? He's coming?"

"Sure. So are your parents, and mine. My sister is away for the weekend, I'm afraid. There will be all different types of people here, Austin."

"And one freak."

"Hey, none of that," he said, pulling her into his arms. "Where's your positive attitude?"

"It's positive. I am positive that I don't want to be at this party." She sighed. "I'm sorry, Sam. It's not fair of me to be so negative. I'll arrive with a smile, I promise." Given a choice, she'd rather spend the evening at the dentist.

"Don't look so sad," he said, lowering his head toward hers. "I really can't handle it when you look so sad."

The kiss was sensational. It made Austin forget

everything except the man who was holding her, and the desire churning within her.

It was two hours later before Austin finally went home.

Her dress was emerald green.

The rich, full-length satin creation did wonderful things for her auburn hair and slender figure, Austin knew, but she didn't really care. The softly draped cowl neckline and wrist-length flutter sleeves lent a deceptively simple elegance to the dress. It was, in fact, quite daring from another view, as her entire back to just above her waist was bare. Her hair was pulled in gentle folds on the top of her head with loose tendrils curling on her neck and next to her cheeks. She looked older, and taller—due to three-inch evening sandals—and actually quite sexy, now that she thought about it.

But she really didn't care.

A knock sounded at the door, Austin sighed, and opened it to Houston. Her eyes widened as he stepped into the room.

"My gosh, Houston," she said, her gaze taking him in from head to toe. "I've never seen you in a tuxedo before."

"I rented it. Not bad, huh?"

"You look like you just stepped out of a fashion magazine, or off a billboard. Gracious, you're gorgeous. Who's your date? She's liable to start tearing your clothes from your body."

"I . . . don't have a date."

"Why not?"

He shrugged. "I don't know. I flipped through my ever-famous little black book, but no one held any appeal. I know what they're going to say before they say it, and they cling, hang on my arm, like they can't stand up alone. I just wasn't in the mood."

"You need a new woman in your life."

He absently ran his finger over the bridge of his nose, then shrugged again. "Ready to go?"

"Yes," she said, turning to pick up her clutch purse.

"Excuse me," he said. "I hate to be the one to break this to you, but someone stole the back of your dress."

"Cute," she said, shooting him a stormy look.

"Poor Sam," Houston said. "You'll have his libido going nuts all evening."

"Poor Sam? Poor Sam!" Austin said none too quietly. Houston jerked in surprise. "What about me? This is the worst night of my entire life."

"Come on," he said, taking her hand. "Let's go to the party. You look sensational, even though half of your dress is missing."

"Exposing my back," she said. "The back being the area between the neck and the end of the spine on the human form. The back is—"

"Austin," Houston interrupted wearily.

"Yes?"

"Shut up."

"I rest my case," she said, then stomped out the door.

"This is going to be one helluva night," Houston said under his breath, then followed Austin out of the apartment, closing the door behind him.

Samuel's house was lit up like a Christmas tree, casting a bright glow of welcome to those who had been invited to join in the festivities. If Houston felt out of place in a tuxedo while driving a pickup truck, then parking said truck between a Mercedes and a Lincoln, he gave no indication of it. Cars filled the driveway and lined the street, with more arriving every minute.

"This is some bash," Houston said as he and Austin walked toward the house. "If I ripped off all the hubcaps and fenced them, I could retire."

"Houston, shame on you," Austin said, trying to sound stern, but then she laughed.

"It's true."

"Have you decided on one of those jobs you've been offered?"

"No, I'm looking around, checking them out. I want to see who's building what these days."

"I'm sorry about Tyler Construction, Houston."

He shrugged. "Yeah, well, someday I might have another shot at it. Besides, that living from paycheck to paycheck wasn't great. I can make darn good money with one of the big outfits. It's time I started thinking of my financial security."

"It is? Why?"

"I'm going to be twenty-eight soon, Austin. I'd like a home, and a . . . forget it."

"Wife? Family?"

He shrugged yet again, but didn't comment.

"I love you, Houston."

"I love you too, kiddo. Well, here we go. Ready?"

"No."

"Austin, Sam loved you. Remember that. Remember it and hold the thought. You two have something special together. Now! Go in there, be Austin Tyler, gorgeous genius, and give 'em hell." He kissed her on the forehead.

"Thank you," she whispered.

He rested his fingers lightly on her elbow and led her to the front door. An instant later it was flung open and Samuel was standing there.

"Hi, Sam," Austin said softly.

"You look"—he cleared his throat—"fantastic. You are the most beautiful woman I've ever seen."

Austin's gaze swept over his perfectly tailored tuxedo, glimpsing the pristine white shirt with the tiny pleats. His shoulders seemed a mile wide, his legs even longer, his arms meant for the purpose of enfolding her into his embrace.

"You're beautiful too," she said. "Really scrumptious."

"Can we come in?" Houston asked.

"Oh," Sam said, tearing his gaze from Austin's, "of course." He stepped back and they entered. He glanced at Austin's dress, then did a double-take. "Austin, where's the rest of your dress?"

"She lost it somewhere," Houston said. "Weird, huh?"

"It's . . ." Sam started, his eyes riveted on her bare skin, "really something."

"I told you you'd shake up the poor guy's libido," Houston said to Austin.

"No joke," Sam said.

"Oh, for heaven's sake," Austin said.

"Looks like things are in full swing, Sam," Houston said. "This is quite a party. House looks great
too."

"Indeed it does," Sam said. "Come on, I'll intro-
duce you to some people."

No! Austin thought frantically. She wanted to
go home. Right now. She did not want to be
there. She was going to faint. She was going to
throw up. She was going to turn around and run
right out that door.

"Austin?" Sam said.

"Yes, I'm coming," she said, forcing a weak smile.

The next fifteen minutes went well. Sam moved
Austin from group to group, making introduc-
tions but not lingering. He kept his arm protec-
tively and possessively around her shoulders.
Houston disappeared on the arm of someone
named Christine, who had the longest eyelashes
Austin had ever seen.

"Uh-oh," Austin muttered as she saw where Sam
was leading her next. That man was a smaller,
older version of Sam. The attractive woman had
Sam's blue eyes. Merciful heavens, she thought,
the jig was up. Those were his parents. That was
the senior Carter, who didn't know how to smile.

"Mom, Dad," Sam said, "I'd like you to meet
Austin Tyler. Austin, my parents, Doris and William Carter."

"Hello," Austin said, extending her hand.

"A pleasure, dear," Doris said, shaking her hand.

"Likewise," William said.

This was it, Austin thought dismally. The final curtain was about to come down. This was the beginning of the end. Oh, Sam.

She drew a steadying breath. Good-bye, Scrumptious Sam. Good-bye, my love. "That's a lovely necklace, Mrs. Carter," she said, amazed her voice was working. "Ivory, isn't it?"

"Yes," Doris said, fingering the dainty charm at her neck. "It was from William on our anniversary last week."

"Oh, really?" Austin said, managing to smile. "Well, that is part of the ritual of the charm."

"I beg your pardon?" Doris said.

"That symbol, while looking simply like an intricate design, is actually more than that. It is associated with the early Egyptians, who had statues erected in its honor. According to custom, a man must give it to his woman in order for the legend, the magic, to work. But since Mr. Carter gave it to you, well . . ." her voice trailed off, and she smiled brightly.

"Just what does it represent?" Mrs. Carter said, her fingers fluttering over the charm.

"Fertility," Austin said. "The man gives it to the woman he has chosen to bear his child. According to ancient records, it somehow seems to have worked splendidly."

Mrs. Carter's mouth dropped open. Mr. Carter turned a strange shade of red. A choking noise came from the vicinity of Sam. Austin smiled pleasantly as a knot tightened in her stomach and her throat ached with unshed tears.

Good-bye, my Sam, she whispered in her mind. There would be no more "Kiss me again, Sam." No more ecstasy as they made love. No more anything. Austin Tyler, genius, had just sealed her fate.

"Well, well," Doris Carter said.

And then to Austin's wide-eyed amazement, Mrs. William Carter burst into laughter. Then Sam Carter joined her. William Carter scowled. Sam and his mother laughed and laughed as Austin watched, her head swiveling back and forth as though she were at a tennis match.

"Oh, how marvelous," Doris said, gasping for breath. She poked William in the ribs with her elbow. "It would serve you right, you old coot, if we had a baby at our age. It would keep you young to do the diaper routine again." Sam hooted in merriment.

"Take that necklace off, Doris," William said, a smile tugging onto his lips. "Good Lord, a fertility charm." He laughed out loud and shook his head. "Young lady," he said to Austin, "you're enough to give a man a heart attack. How on earth did you know about that charm?"

"I . . ." Austin licked her suddenly dry lips. "I'm a genius. I retain everything I read."

"Really?" Doris said. "Heavens, how lucky you are. I have to make lists or I don't remember where I'm supposed to be when. Then I make a list of where I put the lists. It's absurd. Oh, the things I could accomplish if I had your mind."

"This house is one of her accomplishments," Sam said.

"And it's lovely," Doris said. "Sam, would you notice if I kidnapped Austin to organize the Orphan's Ball? Oh, to have someone with a sense of order on my committee."

"Austin could organize order out of any chaos," Sam said. "I've seen her do it. But"—he pulled her close to his side—"yes, I'd notice if you kidnapped her. She's all mine."

"Oh?" William said. "I'll make you a terrific deal on that necklace, son."

"Not a chance," Doris said. "I'm keeping it. I can hardly wait to tell all my friends about this. Austin, you're wonderful. You've certainly added some zest to my evening."

"Heart attack," William said. "Guaranteed."

"Hello, darling," an attractive woman said, kissing Sam on the cheek.

"Sharon," he said, nodding.

"Hello, Sharon," Doris said. "Lovely to see you. Have you met Austin?"

"Sharon McClure," the woman said.

"Austin Tyler," Austin said absently. She had to think, sort this through. Her revelation about the necklace hadn't gone at all as she expected. This was terribly confusing.

"It's Dr. McClure," Doris said to Austin. "Sharon is a surgeon."

"Oh, please," Sharon said, "not tonight. I'm so hoping some gorgeous hunk of man will lust after my body and forget about my mind."

"Austin can probably relate to that," William said. "She's a genius."

"Are you really?" Sharon said to Austin. "Well, not fair. You've also got yummy Samuel. It probably takes a genius to figure out how to have the best of both worlds. You must share your secret with me, Austin. Samuel, who is that incredible specimen over there? The big, broad-shouldered, sexy guy with the auburn hair. Lord above, he's the best-looking thing I've seen in a decade. Except for you, of course, Samuel. But who is he?"

Sam grinned. "That's Houston Tyler, Austin's brother."

"Is he taken?"

"Nope," Sam said.

"Is he a genius too?" Sharon said.

"Nope."

"Oh, goody. We'll forget about minds and concentrate on bodies. Great meeting you, Austin, even though I'm jealous as hell. You're a genius for yourself, and you've got Samuel for the part of you that's just woman. I can't stand it. Okay, Houston Tyler, here I come. Good-bye, all."

"She's exhausting," William said.

"She's refreshing," Doris said.

"She's right," Sam said, looking at Austin. "You have the best of both worlds. Your mind for whatever you want to do, and a man who loves you more than life itself."

"Come along, William," Doris said, taking his arm. "We're not needed here."

"Give Austin the necklace," William said.

"No," Doris said, poking her nose in the air.

"Well, damn," William said as they walked away.

"Austin?" Sam said.

She blinked once very slowly as if coming out of a trance. "What? I don't know what to say. I mean, I thought they'd . . . but they . . . Then Sharon said the best of both worlds?"

"Come with me," he said, taking her hand.

Sam weaved through the crowd, smiling and nodding, then pulled Austin into the kitchen. The catering staff was busily at work, so Sam went farther, taking Austin into the laundry room. He gripped her shoulders and looked directly into her eyes.

"Austin," he said, his voice husky, "listen to me. I realize that you could say that a few reactions to your being a genius aren't enough to base a conclusion on. But, Austin? They are. And do you know why? You've kept your secret ever since you got back from the institute. The last time you told people you were a genius, you were a child, a prodigy. Now? Now you're a mature woman, an adult, being accepted by adults. No, a young girl doesn't fit into an adult society, but a woman does. The best of both worlds, Austin. Your mind and my love, if you want them."

Tears misted Austin's eyes as she looked at Sam, heard the plea in his voice. "Sam? Is it possible? Really possible for me to have the best of both worlds?"

He cradled her face in his hands. "Oh, yes, my darling, it is. Tear down the walls, Austin. Do it. For yourself. For us. I love you! Say it, Austin. Please. Please. Say that you'll marry me."

The greatest calm, the gentlest peace she had ever known settled over Austin. She sifted it through her mind, her heart, then allowed its warmth to touch her soul. Tears spilled onto her cheeks, and a soft smile formed on her lips.

She said one word in a voice no more than a whisper. A whisper filled with serenity and love.

"Yes."

Nine

Sam stood in the darkening room, staring out the window at the light rain that was falling.

Austin was late.

Again.

He turned slowly from the window to glance around the room, remembering the party that had taken place there three weeks before. Sam had called for his guests' attention, then announced that Austin Tyler had agreed to marry him. A cheer had gone up from the throng, followed by hugs, and handshakes, and tears of happiness shed by both Austin's mother and his. Houston had gripped Sam's hand so enthusiastically, he had visions of broken bones, but had survived Houston's overzealous congratulations.

Yes, Sam mused, it had been quite a party, a turning point in his life, a commitment of forever from the only woman he had ever loved. Austin had at last accepted herself as the genius she was, and with that acceptance came the willingness to lower her protective walls and plan a future life with Sam.

Their lovemaking that night, Sam recalled, had been hours long, intense, speaking of their love, their tomorrows, erasing the last doubts and fears. It had been nearly dawn before they'd slept, heads resting on the same pillow.

Austin had moved into his house the next day, and Sam had thoroughly enjoyed watching her place her belongings next to his. The house, he decided, was now a home, because Austin was there to stay.

She did not want, would not have, Austin had stated adamantly, a big, flashy wedding. Judge's chambers would do nicely, she'd like to be a June bride, and since it was now June, there wasn't any problem. They'd gotten their blood tests, the license, and rings, but thus far had not called to get an appointment on the judge's calendar.

To do that, they'd have to decide on a date, Sam thought dryly. And to do *that*, he'd have to see one Miss Austin Tyler. She'd have to actually arrive home when she'd said she could be expected, and once there, be willing to level some attention in his direction.

Samuel sighed and ran his hand over the back of his neck. Three weeks since the party, and so damn much had changed. Austin had not only been welcomed by his circle of friends, she'd been sought after. His own mother had called the day after the party requesting Austin's help in organizing the Orphan's Ball. Soon, the phone had rung off the hook as others asked for her assistance and advice. They weren't just using her intelligence, Sam realized. People sincerely liked Austin, enjoyed her company and enthusiasm.

Why wasn't he happy for her? he asked himself. Hadn't he sincerely wanted her to rid herself of her ghosts of the past and step into a circle of sunshine to discover who she really was? Why wasn't he rejoicing over the way his friends had welcomed her into the fold? Why didn't it warm his heart to see the twinkle in her eyes and the genuine smile on her lips?

Had he felt the power of his own control when Austin had been frightened, wary, when she sought solace in the protective embrace of his strong arms?

Was he, he wondered dismally, a lesser man than he'd imagined himself to be, now resenting her flight from her cocoon of fear to emerge as a lovely, independent butterfly? Did he want her rushing to his arms for protection from the world instead of dashing to eagerly greet all that was beyond their door?

Sam stopped and stood statue-still, listening carefully to the voices of his mind, heart, soul.

The truth was there, among the dark confusion. No, he didn't wish to control Austin's life.

"Thank God," he whispered.

He knew his inner message was true. He knew because when he made love with Austin, he willingly, joyously, relinquished the tight control he held on himself and gave to her completely, took from her completely. Equals. Partners. Man and woman. Sam and Austin. Give and take. One.

And that, he also knew, was how he envisioned their entire life together. He didn't wish to be superior, in control of a frightened woman who clung to him to protect her from those who couldn't accept her level of intelligence.

And now? he thought. She *was* free of the past, *was* like a butterfly flitting from flower to flower in a glorious garden she hadn't known existed. But Samuel had been left at the garden gate to watch her; calling to her, though she didn't hear; beckoning to her, but she didn't come.

Never in his entire life had he felt so lonely.

Again Sam heard the sound of a car, but he didn't move. He felt drained, tired, empty. And cold.

The front door burst open and Austin ran into the room, turning at once to set her wet umbrella back out on the porch before closing the door.

She greeted Sam with a bright smile. "Hi, Sam. Sorry I'm late, but the most exciting thing happened. She placed her purse and a stack of folders on a chair. "I have to go over that material tonight for the Orphan's Ball. It's coming together like clockwork. Anyway, Sharon McClure has a friend who is a psychologist. He wants me to speak to a group of parents of gifted, highly intelligent children. Me! Can you believe that? He wants me to tell them what it's like from the child's point of view, how lonely it can be."

"Lonely?" Samuel said, scowling. "Funny you should use that word."

Austin frowned and crossed the room to look up at him. "Sam? What is it? What's wrong?"

He raked a restless hand through his hair. "You don't know, do you? You can't see it at all."

"See what? I don't know what you're talking about."

"Austin, when are we getting married?" he said, a muscle jumping along his jaw.

"This month, in June, just like we planned."

"Oh, really?" he said, his voice laced with sarcasm. "Have you penciled it onto your busy calendar, subject to change if something else comes up?"

"Sam, what—"

"And when are we going to spend an evening together, providing, of course, you can manage to get here on time. An evening *together*, Austin, not one where your nose is buried in your latest project. Remember dinner? It's that meal at the end of a workday. Thought about sharing one with me lately? I think not."

Austin's eyes widened in shock. "I thought you were happy for me, pleased with the way everything has gone. Ever since the party I've—"

"You've been too damn busy," he yelled, "to devote any time to me and our relationship other than to make love with me. Well, damn it to hell, that's not enough. There's more to me than just the needs of my body, Austin. There's more to us. Or so I thought."

Austin felt the color drain from her face as she

stared at Sam as though she'd never seen him before, as though he were a stranger.

This didn't make sense. What was he saying? Really saying? She had to ask permission to use her abilities, make sure it suited him, didn't upset his routine and almighty control of every situation he was in, including their relationship? What was next? Barefoot and pregnant in the kitchen, dinner on the table the minute he walked in the door?

Just who in the blue blazes did Sam Carter think he was?

"You," she said, planting her hands on her hips, "are out of line, mister."

"Me!" he said, splaying his hand on his chest. "It's a little tough to be out of line when all I do is stand here waiting to see if you'll remember I'm in the room. Oh, and then, of course, I salute as I take off my clothes for my performance in bed every night." Oh, hell, what a tacky thing to say, he thought.

"That," Austin said, her dark eyes flashing with anger, "was the most despicable thing you have ever said."

"Austin, look," he started, his tone gentling as he reached for her, "let's—"

"Don't touch me," she said, taking a step backward. Sam dropped his hand to his side. "I don't understand you, Sam, I really don't," she said, her voice beginning to tremble. "You said you couldn't handle it when I was sad, but now you resent the fact that I'm happy. I've been accepted, I fit in for the first time in my life, and it's by people who are important to you. Why is it all suddenly a threat to you? I have more to offer you, not less. I'm a complete woman within myself, which is how it should be. I come home to you every night feeling fulfilled, worthwhile."

"But," he said quietly, "you don't really come home." He glanced at the stack of folders on the chair, then looked at her again. "You bring it all with you. You're not here, really here, until we go to bed together." He drew a shuddering breath. "It isn't enough."

"What am I supposed to do? Ask your permission to give a speech, be on a committee? Am I to be intelligent only when it's convenient for you?"

"Ah, Austin, no," Sam said, his voice raspy. "I'm asking only that you slow down a little, have a better balance of your time. The best of both worlds, remember? Me, my love, *our* love and future together are starting to get squeezed out of the picture."

"According to *your* measuring stick," she said tightly.

"I *am* half of this relationship, Austin," he said. "I do have a voice. I won't settle for crumbs of time you decide to toss my way. If I didn't know better, I'd begin to think . . ." His voice trailed off.

"Think what? Say it, Sam. What do you think?"

"You've waited all of your life, searched, floundered, and now you've found your place. Maybe being accepted, fitting in, is enough for you."

"No," she said, shaking her head. "No, you're wrong."

Sam's voice was ominously low, flat, when he

spoke again. "Am I?" A shadow of pain crossed over his features and settled in the blue depths of his eyes. "I think"—his voice was thick with emotion—"I think perhaps that's exactly how it is."

"No, no," she whispered, tears spilling onto her cheeks.

"I'm going out for a while," he said, moving past her. He stopped in front of the chair with the folders. "But no problem, right? You have plenty to keep you busy." He started toward the front door.

Austin spun around. "Sam, wait, please. Don't go. I . . ." The door closed behind him with a resounding thud. "Sam?" She heard the sound of his car being driven away. "Sam? Oh, dear God."

On trembling legs Austin made her way to the sofa and sank onto it, pressing her fingertips to her lips, willing herself to stop crying.

There was no time for tears, she told herself frantically. No time for weeping and wailing and feeling sorry for herself. She had to think, sort things through, figure out what had happened, what had gone wrong.

Austin drew a deep breath, then let it out slowly, ignoring the two tears that slid down her cheeks.

Sam knew how much she loved him, she told herself. And he also knew how wonderful it was for her to have found her place among his friends and family. But now he was angry because she was not devoting herself entirely to him. That wasn't fair. He was being selfish, self-centered, determined to bring every aspect of their relationship under his damnable control. Well, ha! No way. No.

"No," she said aloud, lifting her chin. Sam had been giving thought to the word "lonely"? Lonely. Sam? Oh, how well she knew the pain of loneliness, the ache inside as it seemed the world was passing her by as though she didn't exist. Sam was lonely? How could that be when he was about to be married, was the other half of a relationship, was the man to her woman for all time? She came home to him every night. She . . .

Austin turned slowly to look at the stack of folders on the chair, and a chill swept through her. Yes, she admitted, she had planned to work through the evening, just as she had the night before, and the one before that, and countless others in the three weeks since the party. With a feeling of pride and satisfaction she'd set aside her labors at a late hour and rush into Sam's embrace in their bed.

She had been in complete control of their relationship, pushing Sam's buttons, letting him know when it was his turn to be fitted into her busy schedule.

Dear heaven, every accusation Sam had made had been true, she realized. She'd gone berserk. Like a child with a new toy, she'd centered her attention on her newly acquired acceptance, the long-awaited-for knowledge that she fit in. She'd shuffled Sam, their love, their future, around the edges. *She* was the selfish one. In the excitement of being set free of her frightening past, she'd run roughshod over Sam's feelings, his love for her.

She'd had the best of both worlds, and did nothing to nurture the part that was Sam, their relationship, their life together.

She had caused the pain in his eyes.

She had caused the defeat in his voice.

And now he was gone.

"Oh, Sam, I'm so sorry," she said to the empty room. "Come back. Please? Come home and kiss me again, Sam. Please? I'm so, so sorry."

The tears started anew, and Austin made no attempt to stop them. She cried and cried, got the hiccups, and kept on crying. But even as she sobbed, she was listening for the sound of Sam's car telling her he'd come back to her.

But he didn't come.

Hours later exhaustion claimed her, and she curled up on the sofa and slept. Waiting for Sam.

Austin awoke the next morning shortly after eight o'clock, stiff and achy from her hours spent on the sofa. She rushed to the window, and felt a knot tighten in her stomach as she saw that Sam's car wasn't in the driveway.

Where was he? she wondered, walking up the stairs. Was he ever coming back? Well, of course he was, this was his house. He belonged here, but perhaps . . . perhaps he now felt that she didn't. She had to see him, talk to him, tell him he'd been right, and she was so very sorry.

Austin showered, dressed in jeans and a blue cotton top, then phoned Sam's mother and begged off from attending the committee meeting, saying she thought she'd caught cold in the rain the previous night. Mrs. Carter expressed her sympathy and said to have a cup of tea and honey. Austin mumbled her thanks.

And waited for Sam.

Late in the morning Houston called.

"Austin? What in the hell is going on?" he said, not bothering to say hello.

"Going on?"

"Sam showed up at my place last night drunk as a skunk. Before I could find out what his problem was, he passed out cold on my sofa. He was still zonked when I left this morning for work."

"Oh, you've taken a job?" Austin said brightly. "That's nice. Where are you working?"

"I'm filling in as crew chief for a buddy whose wife just had a baby and—Dammit, what's with you and Sam? Spit it out, Austin. I've got to get back on the site."

"Oh, Houston, I made terrible mistakes."

"So, fix them."

"I want to, I'll try to, but I can't do anything if Sam isn't here."

"He'll show up. I left the coffee on Warm and a bottle of aspirin on the end table. He is going to be so hung over, he'll wish he were dead. He was really blitzed."

"And it's all my fault," Austin wailed.

"Jeez, scream in my ear, why don't you? Okay, superbrain, you blew it, so do something about it, whatever it is."

"I love him, Houston," she said, sniffling.

"I know, sweetheart, and he loves you. That's

what's going to make the difference. Good luck. I'll be here if you need me, you know that."

"Thank you. I love you. 'Bye."

" 'Bye, kid."

Austin replaced the receiver and stared into space. So, Sam would show up eventually. And then she'd tell him—

Austin got to her feet. "Not tell," she said aloud. "Show-and-tell. Yes, that's it."

She grabbed her purse and ran out the front door.

To die, Sam had decided upon awakening, would be a blessing.

And with that blurry thought he'd immediately fallen back to sleep.

At four o'clock in the afternoon he surfaced again, stumbled into the bathroom, stripped off his clothes, and showered. He borrowed Houston's razor and shaved, redressed in his wrinkled clothes, and consumed a cup of coffee and two aspirin. He phoned his secretary, apologized for any inconvenience he'd caused, and thanked his lucky stars that his father was out of town and not around to demand an explanation for his failure to show up at work.

Then, deciding he might live after all, he thought about Austin. And thoroughly depressed himself once more. He was losing her, he thought grimly. Losing her to a world she had waited for for all of her life—the world of acceptance. It was bigger, stronger, held greater attraction than his love and what they could plan together for their future.

And he had to let her go.

She was, indeed, like the newly freed butterfly. Austin was too beautiful, too full of life, excitement, the wish to explore all the avenues now open to her, to keep her captive in the circle of his arms. He hated to see butterflies snared in a net, then pinned in place never to fly free again. He couldn't do that to *his* butterfly, his Austin.

He had to let her go.

With a sigh that was more of a moan, he got to his feet, scribbled a note of thanks to Houston, and left the apartment. Feeling like a coward, he decided to go for a drive before returning home and saying good-bye to Austin.

She paced nervously across the living room, stopping often to look out the window for Sam's car. The summer sunset was fading, and darkness was falling like a curtain being slowly lowered to the ground.

She was wearing a burnished gold caftan, and her hair was tumbling down her back. The way Sam liked it.

But, she thought frantically, he'd never see her hair or discover that she didn't have a stitch on under that caftan if he didn't come home.

"Darn it, Sam," she said, "haul your scrumptious tush in here." She heard the sound of a car turning into the driveway. "Oh, good Lord," she said, covering her racing heart with her hand.

A few minutes later Sam walked into the living room. "Hello, Austin," he said quietly. "I'm sorry if you were worried about me."

"Houston called me," she said, searching his face for some clue as to what he was thinking. Nothing.

His gaze swept over her. "You look lovely, fantastic."

"Thank you. Sam, I . . ."

"We have to talk."

"Yes. Yes, we do, but there's something I'd like to show you first. Would you come into the dining room with me? Please?"

He shrugged slightly and nodded, then followed her into the dining room. Austin stepped back so that Sam had a clear view of the table. She drew a deep breath, glanced heavenward, then watched as he walked slowly forward to the edge of the table.

"Sam," she said, her voice trembling, "there's so much I need to say to you, and I will. But I thought I could show you that I understand what I did, how wrong I was, how I got my priorities mixed up because I was so enthralled with all the new things that were happening to me."

He glanced at her, then back at the table.

"You know I was really quite happy up until I went to the institute," she continued. "I owe that happiness to my wonderful family, to the fact that *they* didn't get their priorities mixed up. *They* didn't become enthralled with the fact that I was a genius, they simply treated me like they did any Tyler."

"Go on," he said, looking at her again.

"I didn't use that kind of wisdom with my new gift of acceptance, Sam. I didn't think anything through, I just reacted. I was wrong, terribly wrong, and I hurt you in the process. I'm so very sorry."

"Austin, I—"

"Please, let me finish. I thought about what you had said to me, and I knew you were right. Then, I thought further, back to when I was young, when my family taught me things about acceptance, and priorities, and love, that I never should have forgotten. And so, I'm starting over. I'm at the doorways of the best of both worlds, but this time I'm going to go slowly, wisely, remembering what's important."

She moved to stand in front of him.

"Sam, would you do me the honor of sitting down at this table with me and playing a game of Chutes and Ladders? Would you consider spending a quiet, normal, sharing evening playing a table game with the woman who loves you more than life itself?"

"Oh, Austin."

A sob caught in her throat. "And would you consider forgiving me for hurting you, for being a very dumb genius? Would you"— tears spilled onto her cheeks—"kiss me again, Sam?"

With a moan Sam reached out and grabbed her, hauling her up against him and burying his face in her fragrant hair. A shudder ripped through his body, then he slowly lifted his head. Tears shimmered in his eyes.

"Oh, God, Austin," he said, his voice choked

with emotion, "I thought I'd lost you to that other world. I thought it had more to offer you, things that you wanted more than our life together. I thought I was going to have to let you go . . . like the butterfly. I love you. I will always love you. Yes, I'd be honored to play Chutes and Ladders with you. And, oh, yes, I will kiss you again, and again, and again."

"Starting when?" she said, smiling through her tears.

"Right . . . now."

The kiss was long and powerful, and passions soared. Austin molded herself against Sam, savoring the feel of his aroused body, inhaling his aroma, welcoming the heated desire that swirled unchecked within her. His hands roamed over the silky material of her caftan and she purred in pleasure.

Samuel's head jerked up. "What have you got on underneath this thing?"

She smiled sweetly. "Nothing."

"That's it!" He swung her up into his arms. "I'm out of control and loving every minute of it. I'm taking you to bed, Austin Tyler, where I'm going to make love to you until dawn."

She wound her arms around his neck. "But, Sam, what about our game of Chutes and Ladders?"

"I'll forfeit. You won."

"No, my scrumptious Sam," she said softly, love radiating from her big brown eyes, "we both won."

"And our prize," he said, smiling at her warmly, "is forever. Together."

•   •   •

Miles away, Houston glanced up quickly from the book he was reading, having had the strange sensation that someone had tapped him on the shoulder. He was alone in his apartment.

A slow smile tugged onto his lips, widening into a grin, as he lifted a finger to absently stroke the bridge of his nose.

THE EDITOR'S CORNER

At LOVESWEPT, we believe that the settings for our books can be Anywhere, USA, but we do like to be transported into the lives of the hero and heroine, and into their worlds, and we enjoy it very much when our authors create authentic small town or big city settings for their delicious love stories. This month we'll take you from a farm in Oklahoma, to a resort town on the ocean in New Jersey, to the big cities of Los Angeles, New York, and Chicago, so settle into your favorite traveling armchair and enjoy these new places and new couples in love.

Fran Baker has done a wonderful job recreating the world of the farmer and oilman in **THE WIDOW AND THE WILDCATTER**, #246, a heartwarming and heartwrenching story of love, family, and land. Chance McCoy is a hero you'll love to love. He's strong, gorgeous, adventurous, and available to the woman who needs him to make her and her grandfather's dream come true. What begins as a dream to strike it rich ends as dreams of love are fulfilled for Chance and Joni. Fran Baker certainly does strike it rich in this story!

With our next title, we leave the farmlands of Oklahoma for the New Jersey shore where Cass Lindley, heroine of **SILK ON THE SKIN**, LOVESWEPT #247, owns an exclusive boutique in a resort town, and is the major stockholder of the family's lingerie business. Cass has her hands full of silks, satin, and lace when she discovers that her company is in trouble. M&L Lingerie creates the finest intimate garments for the market but the chairman of the board, Ned Marks, decides they should compete with Fredrick's of Hollywood! Cass is appalled and finally listens to the new president, Dallas Carter, who has a plan to oust Ned. Cass has never mixed business with pleasure but Dallas is too good and too sexy to remain just a professional colleague. They become colleagues in the bedroom as well as the boardroom, pledging a lifelong commitment to each other. Author Linda Cajio has done it again with a sophisticated and sexy love story.

(continued)

Meanwhile, in Los Angeles the subject is real estate, not lingerie. In fact, our heroine is fighting our hero to save her family's ancestral home! **THE OBJECT OF HIS AFFECTION,** LOVESWEPT #248, is another Sara Orwig special. Hilary Wakefield has to resort to dynamite to get Brink Claiborn's attention. It works and the real explosion is the one that happens between them. The gorgeously muscled heartbreaker makes her tremble with smoldering need, and Hilary knows she is flirting with danger by losing her heart to a man she disagrees with on just about everything. But, as usual, Sara Orwig manages to find a common ground for these two lovers who just can't stay away from each other.

January St. John whisks Houston Tyler to an isolated island off the coast of Maine because she's desperate to see the man who stole her heart after only a brief but intense encounter. So begins **JANUARY IN JULY,** LOVESWEPT #249, by Joan Elliott Pickart, and from beginning to end one of your favorite LOVESWEPT authors brings you a love affair to rival any other. January is very wealthy and Houston is a working man—a man who uses his hands and his body in his work and it shows! They come from different worlds but once their hearts touch one another, social differences dissolve. In their island hideaway, they have the opportunity to savor kisses and explore the fireworks that their love creates. They're sensational together, and nothing else matters. Thank you Joan!

LET'S DO IT AGAIN, LOVESWEPT #250, is a first book for us by a new LOVESWEPT author, Janet Bieber. You are all probably familiar with the successful writing team Janet Joyce which has published twenty romances. Well, Janet Bieber was half of that team and now she's gone solo with **LET'S DO IT AGAIN.** So, do give a warm welcome to Janet! I'm sure you're going to enjoy her wonderful story of two lovers who can't let their divorce stand in the way of their love. **LET'S DO IT AGAIN** is about starting over. It's about two adults who have the rare opportunity to learn from their mistakes and build a stronger relationship the second time around. Dave St. Claire returns from traveling the globe determined to

(continued)

convince his ex-wife, Maggie, that they should get rid of that "ex." Dave has realized that a happy family life is really what's important, but meanwhile Maggie has built a life of her own without her wandering husband. But electricity is still there sizzling beneath the surface, and his sweet addictive kisses have grown more potent with time. They get to know each other again, emotionally and physically, and Maggie finally believes his promises. After all, a piece of paper didn't make them stop loving one another!

We end the month appropriately with **THE LUCK OF THE IRISH** by Patt Bucheister, LOVESWEPT #251, a story about trusting and allowing love to grow when you're lucky enough to find it. When Kelly McGinnis first spotted the mysterious woman stepping out of a limousine, he thought of soft music, moonlit nights, and satin sheets! Clare Denham tantalized him with her charm and humor. Clare felt dangerously attracted to the Irishman who had kissed the Blarney Stone and now had powers she couldn't fight. Why fight it when falling in love is the most glorious experience of a lifetime? Patt Bucheister convinced her characters to take the plunge, and I, for one, am glad she did!

We've discovered that in our recent Editor's Corners we accidentally called Kay Hooper's incredible hero, Joshua Long by the wrong last name. I just want to clarify that the dashing and virile Joshua Long is the hero of the "Hagen Strikes Again" series from Kay Hooper.

Enjoy!

Sincerely,

Kate Hartson

Kate Hartson
  Editor

LOVESWEPT
Bantam Books.
666 Fifth Avenue
New York, NY 10103

The first Delaney trilogy

Heirs to a great dynasty, the Delaney
brothers were united by blood, united by
devotion to their rugged land . . . and
known far and wide as

THE SHAMROCK TRINITY

Bantam's bestselling LOVESWEPT romance line built its reputation on quality and innovation. Now, a remarkable and unique event in romance publishing comes from the same source: THE SHAMROCK TRINITY, three daringly original novels written by three of the most successful women's romance writers today. Kay Hooper, Iris Johansen, and Fayrene Preston have created a trio of books that are dynamite love stories bursting with strong, fascinating male and female characters, deeply sensual love scenes, the humor for which LOVESWEPT is famous, and a deliciously fresh approach to romance writing.

THE SHAMROCK TRINITY—Burke, York, and Rafe: Powerful men . . . rakes and charmers . . . they needed only love to make their lives complete.

□ *RAFE, THE MAVERICK by Kay Hooper*

Rafe Delaney was a heartbreaker whose ebony eyes held laughing devils and whose lilting voice could charm any lady—or any horse—until a stallion named Diablo left him in the dust. It took Maggie O'Riley to work her magic on the impossible horse . . . and on his bold owner. Maggie's grace and strength made Rafe yearn to share the raw beauty of his land with her, to teach her the exquisite pleasure of yielding to the heat inside her. Maggie was stirred by Rafe's passion, but would his reputation and her ambition keep their kindred spirits apart?   (21846 • $2.75)

LOVESWEPT

☐ YORK, THE RENEGADE by Iris Johansen

Some men were made to fight dragons, Sierra Smith thought when she first met York Delaney. The rebel brother had roamed the world for years before calling the rough mining town of Hell's Bluff home. Now, the spirited young woman who'd penetrated this renegade's paradise had awakened a savage and tender possessiveness in York: something he never expected to find in himself. Sierra had known loneliness and isolation too—enough to realize that York's restlessness had only to do with finding a place to belong. Could she convince him that love was such a place, that the refuge he'd always sought was in her arms?

(21847 • $2.75)

☐ BURKE, THE KINGPIN by Fayrene Preston

Cara Winston appeared as a fantasy, racing on horseback to catch the day's last light—her silver hair glistening, her dress the color of the Arizona sunset . . . and Burke Delaney wanted her. She was on his horse, on his land: she would have to belong to him too. But Cara was quicksilver, impossible to hold, a wild creature whose scent was midnight flowers and sweet grass. Burke had always taken what he wanted, by willing it or fighting for it; Cara cherished her freedom and refused to believe his love would last. Could he make her see he'd captured her to have and hold forever?

(21848 • $2.75)